LOVE'S CELEBRATION

Teddi's body was draped in white diaphanous gauze, accentuating moonlit dark satin skin and the shadowed womanly crevices of her body.

She dropped the straps and the gown fell to the floor like forgotten cobwebs.

J.T.'s mouth dried as his body responded to her with a rush of heat. How often had he dreamed this?

Then she was in his arms and she was all he ever wanted and needed. His hands and lips moved of themselves, worshipping at the temple of her body.

A whimper emerged from deep within, her eyes dark, bottomless pools.

"How can I live without you?" His words were more a plea than a question.

BOOK YOUR PLACE ON OUR WEBSITE AND MAKE THE ARABESQUE ROMANCE CONNECTION!

We've created a customized website just for our very special Arabesque readers, where you can get the inside scoop on everything that's going on with Arabesque romance novels.

When you come online, you'll have the exciting opportunity to:

- View covers of upcoming books
- Read sample chapters
- Learn about our future publishing schedule (listed by publication month *and author*)
- Find out when your favorite authors will be visiting a city near you
- Search for and order backlist books from our online catalog
- Check out author bios and background information
- Send e-mail to your favorite authors
- Meet the Kensington staff online
- Join us in weekly chats with authors, readers and other guests
- Get writing guidelines
- AND MUCH MORE!

**Visit our website at
http://www.arabesquebooks.com**

LOVE'S
CELEBRATION

Monica Jackson

Pinnacle Books
Kensington Publishing Corp.
http://www.arabesquebooks.com

PINNACLE BOOKS are published by

Kensington Publishing Corp.
850 Third Avenue
New York, NY 10022

Pinnacle, the P logo and Arabesque, the Arabesque logo are Reg. U.S. Pat. & TM Off.

First Printing: December, 1998
10 9 8 7 6 5 4 3 2 1

Printed in the United States of America

We are the children of those who chose to survive.

—*Julie Dash, Daughter of the Dust*

What Kwanzaa Means

Talk by Teddi Henderson at Dixon Junior
High School Auditorium in Dixon, Kansas,
after the Christmas program.

For centuries, African people who lived off the fruits of the land celebrated harvest time with joy and thanksgiving. In 1966, Marcus Karenga, an African-American man, conceived of a holiday people whose ancestors came from Africa and spread into other lands all over the world could celebrate as one united people. The word Kwanzaa is taken from a phrase in an east African language meaning "first fruits" in commemoration of those old African harvest celebrations.

Dr. Karenga envisioned a holiday that celebrated values, principles, family traditions, and community togetherness. He organized the new holiday around five basic activities common to those African first-fruits celebrations. First, the coming together of family and friends, and reverence for the Creator and the creation. Then, remembering the past and the ancestors that traveled before us, and committing again to the values of the African community we sprang from: truth, justice, respect for people and nature, care for the weak and easily hurt, and respect for our elders. And finally, celebrating the good life we have struggled for and achieved. Now, years later, over twenty million people all over the globe celebrate Kwanzaa. They celebrate their beauty and strength as a people and their common roots.

Kwanzaa does not replace Christmas, New Year's, or any other holiday. My family will observe both Christmas and Kwanzaa this year. It's not a religious holiday but rather a time to remember who we are as a people, where we've come from, and where we want to go. It's a time for building up and strengthening our cultural heritage, a time of pride and faith that we try to hold onto throughout the year.

We celebrate Kwanzaa over seven days, December twenty-sixth through January first, and each day is based on one of the seven guiding principles of Kwanzaa: Unity, self-determination, collective work and responsibility, cooperative economics, purpose, creativity, and faith.

Our family has a big wooden box filled with the traditional symbols of Kwanzaa. There is a seven-pronged candlestick that holds the candles we'll light, one for each day. There is a cup that we share to symbolize our unity and that we pour from to symbolize our respect and remembrance of our ancestors. We'll eat special dishes, traditional food from my grandmother's recipes, but also foods from Africa and other lands that African people settled, such as the Caribbean. Our family likes to hear and tell stories. We also exchange gifts. We especially like handmade gifts that hold some special meaning.

We're going to be celebrating the sixth-day Kwanzaa celebration of Karamu on December thirty-first at the Dixon community center. There'll be plenty of food, fun, and tradition. I'm extending an invitation for the entire community to come and bring their family and friends.

Many people have asked why I am inviting European-Americans to a celebration for African-American people. We share this land and this community, and the principles and spirit of Kwanzaa transcend race to call all people to a higher level. African-Americans have celebrated July Fourth for years, although certainly that date had nothing to do with the independence of our ancestors. So join us, and let us make our world and hearts a better place, together.

Nguzo Saba

The Seven Principles of Kwanzaa

1. Umoja (Unity): To strive for and maintain unity in the family, community, nation, and race.

2. Kujichagulia (Self-determination): To define ourselves, name ourselves, create for ourselves, and speak for ourselves instead of being defined, named, created for, and spoken for by others.

3. Ujima (Collective Work and Responsibility): To build and maintain our community together, and to make our sisters' and brothers' problems our problems and to solve them together.

4. Ujamma (Cooperative Economics): To build and maintain our own stores, shops, and other businesses and to profit from them together.

5. Nia (Purpose): To make our collective vocation the building and developing of our community in order to restore our people to their traditional greatness.

6. Kuumba (Creativity): To do always as much as we can, in whatever way we can, in order to leave our com-

munity more beautiful and beneficial than we have inherited it.

7. Imani (Faith): To believe with all our hearts in our people, our parents, our teachers, our leaders, and in the righteousness and victory of our struggle.

The Seven Symbols of Kwanzaa

1. The Mazao: A display of fruits and vegetables to symbolize the harvest. The fruits and vegetables that African people brought and used in their New World are especially appropriate. Teddi displays her Mazao in a basket she bought in Kenya. Cornucopias are inappropriate because of their roots in European traditions.

2. The Mkeka: The mat that holds the Kwanzaa display. The mat is symbolic of our people's foundations. Teddi uses a handwoven rush mat from Africa. Mats of African fabrics are beautiful, or you can use a mat you created, or one created by a family member or a friend would be good.

3. The Mishumaa saba: Seven candles which are lit in turn through the seven days of Kwanzaa. One candle is black, symbolizing our people, three are red for the struggle without which there would be no future, symbolized by three green candles. The black candle is in the middle, the red candles to the left, and the green candles to the right. On the first day of Kwanzaa the black candle is lit, then on each day, the candles are lit alternately from left to right.

4. The Kinara: A candle holder that symbolizes our ancestors, often with an African design or feeling, and handmade. Not a Jewish menorah, it has seven branches, each of which holds one of the Mishumaa

saba. Teddi's kinara is wooden and intricately carved with African designs.

5. The Muhindi: Ears of corn, each of which symbolizes a child in our family. Corn represents continuity, as each ear bears the seeds that can grow into other stalks producing other ears with the potential to propagate to infinity and eternity. Teddi has one ear of dried Indian corn that she bought when her daughter was born.

6. The Kikombe cha umoja: A communal cup symbolizing the unity of all people of African descent. The cup is passed around the gathering and a libation called tambiko is poured to the east, west, north, and south to honor our ancestors.

7. The Zawadi: Zawadi means the gifts. Gifts are exchanged in accordance with the family preference, whether a few on each day of the holiday, or all on one particular day. Teddi and her family always exchange gifts all at once on the seventh day of Kwanzaa, a day they celebrate together as a nuclear family. The gifts are chosen keeping our roots and purposes in mind and utilizing the principles of Kuumba, creativity, and Ujamma, cooperative economics. Teddi likes to order some gifts from African-American-owned companies.

Greetings for the Seven Days of Kwanzaa

For the seven days of Kwanzaa, greetings are made in Swahili. *"Kwanzaa yenu iwe naheri"* means "Happy Kwanzaa." *Harambee* means "Let's pull together." *"Habari gani?"* means "What's happening?" The response is the principle of the day.

Prologue

The day had started like any other day. The timer on the TV was set and Teddi woke to the voice of the weatherman forecasting a cold but sunny December day. J.T., as usual, had buried himself deeper under the covers.

"Wake up, hon," she whispered. "It's almost time to get ready for work."

"Good mornin', love," he rumbled, his voice still heavy with sleep. He leaned over and kissed her tenderly, lingering on her lips. Married for six years, they'd long since passed the point of worrying about morning breath and A.M. dishevelment.

"What time is it?" J.T. asked.

"Too late for what I know you have in mind."

He chuckled. "We'll make the time," he said, his hand gliding under the old T-shirt she wore to sleep in.

"I have to go to the bathroom," she whispered.

"So do I," he whispered back.

Suddenly she pushed off the covers and raced to their adjoining bathroom, with J.T. hot on her heels. She reached the door first. "You lose," she said, laughing, and shut the door on him.

She heard him lean on the door. "You've got to come out of there sometime, and justice awaits."

Teddi giggled, then thought of how blessed she was. She had a wonderful husband who she loved madly and who was crazy about her, and a beautiful five-year-old daughter who'd just started kindergarten. They had it all, a lovely home in Connecticut, and J.T. had an excellent job as a computer salesman in New York. When she got pregnant with Sylvie, they'd made the decision together that she would stay home with the baby.

She was supremely content with her life. Her marriage was as solid as any other marriage she'd seen or heard about. She trusted J.T. implicitly, and it seemed as if their love expanded with every passing day instead of growing routine or stale. They were part of each other and she couldn't imagine doing without J.T. any more than she could imagine doing without her heart.

"Baby, you still alive in there?" J.T. called.

"I'll be out in a second."

She flushed the toilet and turned on the shower. Dropping her clothes to the floor, she got into the stall. "Come on in," she called.

"May I join you?" J.T. soon asked.

"I was counting on it," Teddi purred.

She caught her breath at the magnificence of his body. She'd never gotten used to it, or taken J.T.'s male beauty for granted. Six feet and three inches of toned and muscled African-American manhood, his brown, chiseled features were also strikingly handsome. Women turned in the street to look after him. She'd never met a man so unassuming about his good looks. When someone commented on them, he'd just shrug, embarrassed, and change the subject. And he was so sweet to her; he paid attention to everything she said, and was expressive, affectionate, and funny. J.T. oozed intelligence and strength.

Unlike herself, J.T. was anything but average. Occasionally she'd catch a sister looking at her with that assessing look in her eye, wondering what she had to catch and hold a man like J.T.

Sometimes she wondered herself. J.T. told her that when he first met her, he simply liked her more than he'd ever liked another woman. Then when he found out how hot she was, that was it—he had to have her, he'd said, laughing.

Teddi was average height and weight with a medium-toned complexion, and medium-length hair. Her features, while regular and pleasing, didn't stand out. Her style was quiet, classic, a little reserved. Yes, the word average described her.

But she, Teddi Henderson, had it all, and she made a point to thank God every day for her blessings and to give whatever and whenever she could.

J.T. reached for her. She put out a hand. "My turn first," she said, and slathered soap on his body, lingering on those sensitive special areas until his breath came fast.

"Now, my turn," he said, taking the sponge and soap from her. Soon, her world narrowed to the touch of his hands, the feel of his body, and the aching within her that begged to be filled.

Later, she drew on her robe, as satisfied and sated as any woman could be, and went to get her daughter up and put breakfast on the table while her husband dressed for work.

Sylvie was buried under the covers just like her dad when he really didn't want to get up. "Sweetie, it's time," she said, gently shaking her daughter's shoulder.

Sylvie turned over and stared at her mom with big brown eyes. "What are we having for breakfast this morning, Mama?" she asked. That had always been Sylvie's first question of the day since she could talk. Teddi suspected the anticipation of breakfast served as a boost to get her out of bed.

"A cheese and ham omelet, with hash browns on the side and fresh fruit," Teddi said. "Milk, too," she added.

"We always have milk, Mama," Sylvie said with a grin.

"I laid out your clothes, sweetie," Teddi called as she went to get breakfast started.

She was pouring the hot coffee into mugs when J.T. came down the stairs adjusting his tie.

"Smells good," he said. Sylvie was already at the table. Teddi slipped into her chair, the steaming platters of food were in front of them, and they lowered their heads.

"Lord, thank you for this day of life, our health, and the abundance we enjoy, including this food before us. Above all, thank you for my wonderful daughter, and this woman at my side, without whom I would be incomplete. Amen."

Teddi smiled at him as she picked up her mug of coffee. No, she couldn't imagine God blessing her more than he had already.

But it was a small blessing that she didn't realize then that would be the last time she sat at that breakfast table with J.T.

One

Every shut-eye ain't sleep and every goodbye ain't gone.

—*Traditional*

Teddi Henderson was spreading the woven rush mat over the table she was setting up for Kwanzaa when she heard a crash from the basement. She hesitated a moment, then bent back down over her wooden box of Kwanzaa keepsakes.

Every item in that box was handmade, full of meaning and rife with memories. Her eyes filled with tears and she stood up, thinking about going down to the basement to investigate the sound, knowing she was only prolonging handling the items her family once had cherished. The sound was probably nothing. She'd been jumpy ever since J.T. . . .

J.T. Even thinking his name still caused pain. Teddi closed her eyes. It still hurt so bad. Two years passing had hardly dulled the sharp edges. And now on the eve of Kwanzaa, with the Christmas festivities over and the holiday that J.T. had loved most about to start—now, the pain flashed fresh, the knife still cutting into her heart. And the memory made it feel as if that terrible day was happening all over again . . .

Two years ago, on the day school let out for Christmas, she'd picked up her daughter, Sylvie, in their Jeep Cherokee. As they turned onto their street, Sylvie's happy chatter fell to silence as they saw the fire trucks and emergency vehicles crowding their street. Fear struck Teddi when she realized that they were all in front of her house.

She'd told Sylvie to wait in the car and stumbled through the crowd to the men who surrounded the smoldering ruin that used to be her home. Then she saw the ambulance, and the covered body the attendants were loading.

She broke through the line, running, not making a sound, the fear clutching her heart so great she could scarcely breathe. They had stopped her then. She choked out who she was, then the hard grips holding her back loosened, and their voices grew heavy with sympathy. A male had been pulled from the charred ruins of the house. His body was unrecognizable. She wouldn't want to see him, they said.

Not see J.T.'s white teeth gleam in the smile that slowly and frequently broke out in his ebony face? Not ever feel his arms around her, his strong body? She couldn't imagine it. In the last eight years of her life, every morning when she woke, she first thanked God for his blessings, chief of which was this wonderful man and child she'd been given. And now they were telling her he was gone.

Her parents flew in to take her home. They all stayed at a hotel during the few days it took to finish up the business of closing out the part of her life that mattered most to her. Except Sylvie. She still had Sylvie, Teddi reminded herself.

She never quite believed J.T. was gone. Wouldn't she

feel it if J.T. was no longer in the world, a part of her torn away? But, there she was, whole, and unsundered. Only her world had turned to shades of gray. She felt as if she no longer existed, a mere wraith drifting on the outskirts of human activity.

Sylvie had reverted to babyhood, not wanting to leave her arms. Teddi would sit in the upholstered rocker by the hotel window, holding her daughter, afraid something would snatch her away as abruptly and as finally as J.T. had left her life. Teddi had rocked Sylvie, and they'd exchanged murmurs of shared grief and love. She'd thought that was as bad as it would get. But it got worse.

The detectives came and told her that two men had died in the fire and neither was her husband. Her husband was missing, and with him, a large amount of money was missing from his company. Teddi didn't want to hear any more.

Weeks later, a letter arrived at her parents' home with a New York postmark and no return address.

"Baby, I had to go. Please don't search for me. I want you to leave town and start over. Check our savings account. Kiss Sylvie for me and believe I'll love you both always. Goodbye."

J.T. had deposited more in their savings account than she ever thought he'd earned in his job as a computer salesman. All the things she once believed about her marriage and her life crumbled into dust. She'd never, ever understand.

Confusion replaced her grief, and over time her confusion became edged with anger. How could he? How dare he be alive somewhere without her? She wished he were dead. Then she'd give anything to have him back. Loving him was agony, and hating him was exquisite torture. But the bottom line was that J.T. was gone.

When a second letter arrived with a New York postmark and no return address, she tossed it into a file. She'd open it later. Right now, she couldn't bear the hurt any additional revelations would cause. The bottom line was that J.T. was gone. Nothing was going to change that. She had a daughter, and shreds of a life. She'd have to see past her pain and pick up and go on.

When things get real bad, home is where you run. Teddi had never thought she'd return to the little town in Kansas where she'd been raised. As soon as she graduated from high school, she'd gone off to college as far from Kansas as she could get, in the biggest, baddest place she could think of: New York City. She'd met J.T. in Manhattan, and right away they'd fallen in love with no holds barred and no hesitation. Life was perfect. Too perfect.

When she got pregnant, they'd left the city for a house in Connecticut. She'd stopped teaching to be a full-time mom to her daughter. Sylvie was the light of their lives, rounding out the fullness of their marriage. Soon, Teddi longed for a second child. J.T.'s eyes had lit up when she'd mentioned it to him, then they became strangely shuttered. Not now, he'd said. Maybe later. Later had stretched out to years.

Sylvie was seven now. Teddi taught eighth-graders at the school she had once attended. The kids were rambunctious and bursting with hormones, but she loved it. Teaching was in her blood and she hadn't realized how much she'd missed it. Dixon, Kansas, was a far cry from the mean streets of NYC where she used to work. But teaching was teaching, and she had so much to share with these children.

She'd been shocked at how little African and African-American history was included in the teaching curriculum. She'd planned workshops and education programs for Black history week, and hopefully they would stay in place throughout the year. She'd added black to the colors of Christmas to decorate for Kwanzaa. Black was the color of her people, red the color of the blood they had shed, and green for the Motherland they had sprung from.

She was getting an uneasy reception, especially when she'd started talking about the Kwanzaa celebration. Most people thought it was outlandish, and a few parents even complained to the school board about a teacher promoting "pagan, unchristian rites." Conversations of some of the other teachers stopped when she entered the teachers' lounge. Teddi didn't care.

Pulling herself back to the present, she sighed as she reached for the kinara, the Kwanzaa candle holder, from the box. There was still such a long way for her people to travel. Teddi remembered how it was for her growing up in a place that didn't recognize the beauty and strength of her color and culture. She wanted better for her daughter, for this generation of African-American children. There weren't many in this area, but she wanted them to be instilled with just as much pride in their heritage as the white kids were. If it made her unpopular in this town, a hometown girl returned with fancy big-city ways and ideas, so be it.

The house seemed chilly, and she rubbed her hands along her arms. The thermostat was fine. A feeling of deflation filled her as she stared at the Kwanzaa table. She told herself it was the inevitable Christmas letdown. But it was more than that.

Teddi wanted to get the Kwanzaa table set up before Sylvie came home, but she could hardly bear the memories. She hugged herself and wished Sylvie was here, but she was still at Teddi's parents' house, playing with her cousins in town.

Christmas had been wonderful, with her brother and his family there, and her sister in from Kansas City. But it was Kwanzaa that Teddi anticipated this year, the first she'd celebrated since J.T. had left. Last year she couldn't bring herself to celebrate the holiday J.T. loved the most. The wounds had been too fresh, the pain too raw.

A step creaked and Teddi froze. It was the seventh step up from the basement. That step always creaked, but it'd never seemed important enough to have repaired. Oh, God, was someone in the house with her? Maybe it was nothing—the settling of the house, her nerves.

Teddi moved quickly and soundlessly to her desk in the living room. She sat down and listened intently. There was silence, but hairs stood up at the base of her neck. Someone was in the house with her. How was it that she was so certain? Was it the scent of sweat or the beating of a heart she detected through senses older and more primal than the ones she usually relied on?

She eased a gun out of the desk drawer, took the bullets out of another drawer, and efficiently loaded the weapon. She'd always had mixed feelings about guns. J.T. wanted to make sure she knew how to handle one. Out on the shooting range, they'd both been astonished at how good she'd been. But she'd never wanted to keep one in the house, especially with a small child. After J.T. left, that had changed.

She knew she'd use this gun if she had to, and use it well. She should get up and search the house, but something held her back. Drawing the phone close to her, she wanted to call for help, but what could she say? A stair creaked and woman's intuition had told her there was danger? The police would laugh themselves silly.

Suddenly the air in the room changed. She knew someone was close. Her hand tightened convulsively on the gun. She moved toward the hall. Was he alone? She didn't think two men could be so silent. Christmas was always the most dangerous time of year with its emphasis on buying and having. If you didn't have, you wanted, and from there it was easy to make the leap to taking. She wished she'd never procrastinated on having a security system installed, but here in Dixon, Kansas, she didn't believe it was that necessary.

The floor creaked, toward her bedroom. Teddi crept down the hall toward the sound, scarcely breathing.

A black male, tall and well built, was sitting on her bed staring out the window at the new fallen snow. His back faced her.

"Freeze," she said, cursing herself the moment the word left her mouth. She'd always thought that was a stupid thing to say when she heard it on TV. Any fool could see the man wasn't moving.

She remembered what J.T. had told her so long ago. *When in danger, never hesitate, honey, act. That second of hesitation could cost you your life.*

"Turn around real slow and keep your hands out or I swear to God, I'll put a bullet through you."

He turned slowly. Her eyes widened.

"Teddi," he started to say.

Then the gun jumped in her hand, seemingly of its own volition, and fired. The report was unbearably loud in her ears. He moaned and crumpled off the bed to the floor, clutching his leg.

Teddi stared down at him in disbelief, her heart pounding. She'd just shot her husband, J.T.

Two

Everything we see is a shadow cast by that which we do not see.

—*Martin Luther King. Jr.*

J.T. clutched his leg, warm, wet blood leaking through his fingers. He glared at her. "You knew it was me before you shot," he accused.

Teddi nodded, feeling dazed. She took refuge in practical things, not trusting herself to speak what her mind screamed. "I better call an ambulance, you need to get to a hospital. Can you stand?"

"No hospital," J.T. said, his voice strained. "Help me into the bathroom. I think it's just a flesh wound." He stared at her. "I haven't forgotten what a good shot you are, you could have really hurt me if you wanted to."

"I probably should have killed you." Teddi trembled, her emotions so rampant they threatened to explode through her skin.

"You can put down the gun now," J.T. said, eyeing her.

She didn't move. "Teddi, you can put the gun down now," he said again, his voice gentler.

She raised the gun and he flinched. Teddi got a perverse feeling of satisfaction at his movement.

"I can explain everything," he said, eyes on the gun.

"Don't bother," Teddi said, as the shock wore off and anger too long denied rushed up within her. "I should shoot you again."

A weary expression crossed J.T.'s face. He rubbed his eyes. "Maybe so, but please don't."

Teddi noticed the new fine lines on his features, the dark smudges under his eyes. Most of all she noticed a different air about him. Was it bone weariness and defeat? That wasn't like him. J.T. never quit on anything, he never gave up. He'd worry a problem like a dog with a bone until he'd solved it. Suddenly overwhelming depression filled her and she lowered the gun.

A long low exhalation of relief came from J.T. The blood puddled in a dark spot on the beige carpet under his thigh. "Help me up, Teddi," he said. "Please," he added.

Teddi helped him up, not letting go of the gun. He leaned heavily on her as they made their way to the bathroom. She tried not to watch as J.T. stripped his T-shirt off. He winced as he pulled his jeans down, losing his balance and falling against the wall as he pulled the denim away from his injured leg. It took all Teddi's willpower not to run and help him.

The muscular contours of his hard, brown body were as firm and toned as ever, maybe a little leaner. He turned on the shower and stood in the hot water, steam rising, and blood from the wound in his leg going down the drain. "It's a minor wound, very shallow," he said. "The bullet went right through my outer thigh, just beneath the skin."

He turned off the water and looked at her. "Would you get some Betadine, if you have it, and something to use as a bandage?"

Teddi nodded and started to turn. Then she frowned and raised the gun again, pointing it unerringly between his eyes.

"Why, for God's sake, why did you run out on me like that? Don't you realize what I went through?" Her voice quavered.

Sadness filled J.T.'s eyes. "I had no choice, baby. I couldn't see my family hurt."

She flipped the safety back off the gun. His eyes widened. "Another woman then? You no-good son of a bitch. I could kill you right here and now and no one would be the wiser."

"No, not another woman, never any women but you, my love."

He pushed the gun to the side and hopped out of the shower with his good leg, wincing a little. He wrapped a towel around his waist in a smooth motion.

"I'm going to let you know why I had to leave, but first let me take care of this leg."

She looked away from him, confusion overriding her anger. Turning to the cabinet where she kept her medications and supplies, she threw it open. Then she ran out of the room. Teddi threw herself on her bed, finally releasing the gun. She wanted to cry and scream, but her eyes remained dry. She curled into a ball, and squeezed her eyes shut.

Then she felt the mattress depress as he sat by her. J.T. had entered the room soundlessly. He always moved like a cat. She used to call him her black cat because he was sleek, smooth, and cool. She'd always thought black cats were good luck for her until two years ago when she'd discovered better. He reached over her and took the gun, fixing the safety.

"Baby, I had to go," J.T. said again. "There was no other way out. They'd killed my partner, Paul, and tried to kill me. They threatened you and Sylvie. The crap was too deep, and I had to cut loose. I couldn't protect my family and I was afraid."

She'd never imagined J.T. admitting he couldn't protect his family or that he was afraid. But he was right about one thing, the crap was deep.

She sat up and stared at him. He was dressed in gray sweatpants and a matching hooded jacket. He looked like a thug.

"Who are *they*?" she asked. "You're the one with a warrant for your arrest for embezzlement. When the police catch up with you, they'll probably charge you with Paul's death also. Was it worth it, J.T.? Was the money worth killing your friend and abandoning your family?"

Pain filled J.T.'s eyes and he looked away. He started to speak, but the words caught. Long seconds ticked by.

He finally cleared his throat and looked at her. "What kept me going these long months was the thought of you. Somehow I knew that you'd always trust in me, and believe that I could do none of those things. In my heart I knew that our love was stronger than anything, and nothing could destroy it."

Confused, her emotions warred, yearning and anger, hurt and bewilderment, fear and desire. Anger won. Teddi had yet to hear him take any responsibility for what he had done to her, and to Sylvie. She waited, not trusting herself to speak.

"There are things about me that you never knew. I did what I had to do," he said.

That was it. Teddi exploded upright and swung her hand against his cheek with all her strength. She wanted to scream every foul cussword ever invented at him and even that wouldn't be satisfying enough. How dare he dismiss two years of agony with "I did what I had to do." Damn straight there were things she didn't know about him. Like what he had done with the three million dollars they said were missing.

She drew back her hand to swing at him again, but he grabbed her and pulled her against him. The feel of his warm, so familiar body against hers shocked her into stillness.

"I'm so sorry, baby. There's nothing I can say to make it better, is there? I'm so sorry I let this happen to us," he said.

And at those words Teddi felt the pain cut within her like a sharp knife and she gasped at its intensity. Tears filled her eyes and sobs filled her throat.

J.T. rocked her back and forth, crooning the love-words he'd murmured to her so long ago. Pleasure and pain flooded through her, cradled in those arms she'd thought would never hold her again. If only time could be rewound to three years past when things had been right, and their love had flamed fierce and strong.

"I never was a computer salesman," he said. Teddi pulled back and looked at him.

"I worked for the NIA, a government agency, since we've been married. My position was classified and the computer job was my cover."

"You're telling me you lied to me for years?" Teddi asked, her voice rising.

"I couldn't tell you. It would have put you in danger."

"Then you'd have to kill me," Teddi said bitterly. "That's what they say in the movies right? You told me you were out of the cloak-and-dagger business, that you couldn't deal with it anymore. You told me you'd die before you'd kill again."

"It was an office job, Teddi, even though it was a classified position. I monitored possibilities of terrorist activity. There was nothing dangerous about it. I sat in front of a computer all day."

"So why do you come breaking into my home after

disappearing for two years without a word? Until I got that sorry note you left me, I thought you were dead." Teddi's body stiffened and her eyes narrowed. "There's nothing more you can say to me. I'm calling the police right now so they can lock your lying butt up where it belongs." She slid off the bed and crossed the room to the phone.

"No." J.T. moved swiftly behind her and caught her shoulder. She whirled at him, her hand poised to strike at him again. She stopped at the sight of his eyes. She'd never seen them look so sad, like black pools reflecting only misery.

"No," he repeated softly. "It would put you and Sylvie in danger if they found out where I am." J.T. rubbed his eyes. "It was insanity to come here, but I missed you both so much. Is Sylvie at your parents'?"

Teddi didn't want to, but she nodded.

"I want to see her badly, but it would be best if I go now," he said, taking a long look at Teddi, appearing to drink in the sight of her.

"I'll always love you Teddi, Sylvie, too," he said, his voice a mere whisper. J.T. limped to the front door, and reached for the doorknob.

"Wait." Teddi couldn't let him go like this, couldn't let him walk out of her life again. She crossed the room and put a hand on his arm. "Tell me the truth, J.T. You owe me that."

He sighed, but he couldn't hide the relief that brightened his eyes. He walked over to the sofa, sitting down. Teddi stood, still stiff.

"Paul ran across something that interested him. Large shipments of guns were being diverted from a factory, and we couldn't trace them. This is the kind of thing we were alert for. Then I came across evidence that the guns were slated for the Baltic. I told Paul to forget it, but he said it looked fishy and kept digging."

"I didn't think any more about it until a few weeks later when he drew me aside and said he had evidence that Leland, our immediate supervisor, was diverting the guns to the inner city.

"What Leland was doing wasn't exactly illegal, unless they were automatic weapons. But it was immoral. I confronted him with it, and he shrugged, neither denying nor confirming it."

"If it wasn't illegal, what did it matter to you?" Teddi asked.

J.T. shot her a look. "You've been out of Kansas long enough to know what it's like. There's never a shortage of twenty-dollar guns, no grocery store for miles, but a liquor store on every corner, crack, and other drugs from South America and Asia are cheap and plentiful. Funny, how I never saw no homeboys sporting airplanes or boats to get that stuff over here. I've never seen any gun factories smoking in our neighborhoods. Where is all this stuff our people are destroying themselves with coming from?"

Teddi nodded, impatient. "But what does this have to do with us?"

"Paul wouldn't let it go. The idea of somebody funneling guns into African-American neighborhoods for their personal priorities burned him. Then, Paul left a message on my voice mail saying that he was on to something and it was bigger than I could imagine. He said he needed my help and to meet him for lunch. That was the last time I ever heard from him."

"Your point?" Teddi asked, still impatient.

J.T. frowned at her. "I waited for him at the park where we were to meet and two guys forced me into a car at gunpoint. They drove me around, wanting to know what Paul had found out and what he'd told me. I couldn't convince them I didn't know anything," he said.

"Then they threatened my family." J.T.'s voice qua-vered. "They took me home to wait for you and Sylvie to arrive. They took great pleasure in describing exactly what they were going to do, first to you, than to Sylvie, to make me talk.

"I couldn't let it happen, Teddi." He clenched his fists and the dark, raw pain filled his eyes again.

He looked down at his hands, the hands Teddi knew had seen too much blood in his lifetime, the hands he'd sworn never to use to shed blood again.

"You killed them," Teddi said. She was one of the few people in the world who knew J.T.'s history. She didn't doubt that he was capable of killing two armed men holding him hostage, but she also knew what it had cost him. Teddi wondered who'd sent only two men to contain J.T.? Whoever it was didn't know him too well.

"Did you burn the house?" Teddi asked.

"No. I went back to the office. I needed to find Paul, to find out why those men were after me. Leland was nowhere to be found, and when I walked in the office silence fell over the place. Then I saw a group of men coming and I knew they were coming for me."

J.T. paused and looked away from her. "I cleared out. I went under and tried to get in touch with my old contacts. Nothing. It was as if I was dead already. I went to Washington. Finally I made contact with a man I used to work for, an old friend who owed his life to me. He told me to go deep and stay deep. He said all he could give me was assured protection for you and Sylvie, but only if I disappeared. He said Paul and Leland were dead."

Teddi chewed the inside of her cheek. "What would your old contact have to do with what happened? And why would he give us protection?"

"That's what I've spent the last two years trying to

find out, trying to find out what Paul knew, trying to find anything that would free me to claim my life."

"So why did you come back now after all this time?"

J.T. shook his head. "Maybe I should have waited, but I needed my family. I need you. This time of year is so hard. I thought the missing would get easier with time. It doesn't. It gets worse."

"I know," she whispered.

"Every time I close my eyes I see you, Teddi. I just couldn't be without you anymore."

Unbidden, tears rolled down her cheeks. She wiped them away, ashamed of her weakness. She didn't tell J.T. that she still prayed wordlessly every night for a miracle, for him to be with her and all to be right again with her world.

Then J.T. gathered her into his arms, and the dust motes froze in the air, and the pause between Teddi's heartbeats became endless. And right then for that one moment, J.T.'s arms enfolding her were all that mattered.

Three

I been in sorrow's kitchen and licked out all the pots.
—*Zora Neale Hurston*

J.T. pulled away first. "My family's and your safety matters more than anything else to me."

Teddi said nothing, not wanting to return to the doubts and uncertainties that she faced outside of J.T.'s arms.

"I promised that I would lie low, so it would look as if I were dead to the world in return for your and Sylvie's continued safety. He's kept his side of the bargain."

"Who would try to harm us? I haven't seen anything that would have me believe . . ."

"You wouldn't. Whoever sent those men to kill me, whoever had Paul and Leland killed has a very large stake in me not talking about whatever Paul turned up. I'm in the dark here. Not only don't I have the information they think I have, I don't even know who they are. The man who assured my family's protection is a man I used to work for. A man I trust implicitly, but a man who is not about to talk about anything he doesn't absolutely have to."

Teddi sat down heavily on the couch. Her head was spinning. It was too much. The simple fact that J.T. was back in her life was stunning, but what J.T. was telling her on top of it was almost too much to absorb. A suspicion struck her.

"What about the money?" she asked.

"I don't know. The money I gave you was money I'd squirreled away from when I worked with Special Task Forces. As far as the money I supposedly embezzled from the so-called company I used to work for, that was a setup to bring me in. The company is merely a cover for the arm of the NIA that I was working for."

"I thought you said you'd gotten out of the spy business. Why didn't you tell me?"

"I did get out of the work that I thought put me at risk. And due to the highly classified nature of my work, my silence was a condition of my employment."

"If you wanted a desk job, you could have gone into civilian work."

J.T. sighed. "It wasn't all that easy. What I do best is not a skill in high demand in the civilian economy," he said drily. "When I was offered this job, it seemed the perfect solution since I was given the opportunity to acquire skills in computers that I didn't have."

"What now, J.T.? There's a warrant out for your arrest, and you say that if it's found out you're here that we'll all be in danger."

"I think I know who's responsible for this mess and why. I need to finish what Paul started. I believe Paul had the key to bring it all down, I just have to get it."

"You told me Paul was killed, and they tried to kill you on the mere suspicion that you knew what Paul found out. How are you going to finish what he started without getting yourself killed?"

J.T. gave a wolfish grin. "I'm a lot better than he was," he said.

Sheer nervousness started Teddi pacing. She paused in front of the Kwanzaa table and caressed the sculpture they'd bought in Kenya.

Teddi turned to him, her eyes glistening with unshed tears. "It's all or nothing isn't it? That's why you came back now. Either you finish what Paul started or you die. And the odds against you are high, aren't they?"

J.T. limped closer to her, wiping the single tear that spilled on her cheek with a gentle hand. "I will have my family back. I waited two years. I've left evidence that I'm dead even to my friend in Washington. I'm not going to fail, baby. I hoped to spend the seven days with you, then do what I have to do. I love you, Teddi. I'll spend the rest of my life trying to make up for this."

"From what you tell me it sounds as if the rest of your life isn't going to be that long. How can there be love without trust?"

With those words, Teddi turned away from him and went into the kitchen. She took the plastic grocery bag filled with attractive fruits and vegetables to adorn the Kwanzaa table. She went back into the living room under J.T.'s watchful eyes and started to arrange them in a basket with a woven-in-African pattern. Their silence was pregnant and heavy with unsaid words.

"When is Sylvie coming back?" J.T.'s voice broke the silence like the sound of shattering glass.

"I don't know. She's at my parents'." Teddi paused, frowning. "Did you ever think about how your sudden reappearance would affect Sylvie? Or did you only think of yourself?" she asked.

"You and Sylvie are all I've thought of for two years. I've decided to be honest with her," he said.

"You've decided! You weren't honest with her when you walked out of her life. How dare you breeze in thinking you have the right to make that decision. Her memory of you has faded. How is her daddy rising from the dead going to affect her?"

"I don't know. But I think being straight with her is what I should do. It's early to learn that life can be hard and unfair, but it's still a lesson she will have to learn eventually. I want these seven days with my family. And then . . . if it's what you want, Teddi, I'll clear out of your life. But we had a good marriage, the best. You cannot believe that I'd throw it all away on anything less than life or death."

No, she didn't believe that. She accused him of not trusting her, but how could she trust him not to walk out of her life again after she'd let him back into her heart? He was standing too close to her, reaching a hand out to touch the kinara, the cup, the sculptures that held so many memories. Teddi's heart started to pound, and she took a step backward.

"Do you want something to eat?" she heard herself asking.

J.T. nodded, not looking away from the table.

Teddi moved to the kitchen and mechanically got out pots and pans. The only thing thawed was chicken. She'd fry it the way J.T. liked it. Her hands fell into the comforting rhythms of the kitchen, chopping, washing, mixing, and stirring. The kitchen was always the heart of her home and her refuge when she was troubled. There was something about preparing a meal for someone she loved that calmed her soul and soothed her mind.

Someone she loved. Maybe she'd loved J.T. too hard and too much for him not to be taken from her. Maybe the gods did grow jealous. Maybe she hadn't been good enough for things to have been so right. The knife slipped and bright red blood appeared. An omen? She sucked her finger and her eyes burned from more than the fumes from the onion.

Now, J.T. was back with tales of danger and intrigue. He had brought her dearest wish and worst fear with him. She'd wanted her family back so badly it hurt, but the pain of what she believed was J.T.'s betrayal hurt more. Did she trust him? She'd flung the words at him that without trust there was no love, but did she believe it herself? The Lord knew she loved the man, but she didn't trust him out of her sight. He'd hurt her too much and all his glib answers just made her want to ask more questions.

Despite everything, she'd always known he was alive somewhere. She'd have whispered conversations with him on those endless nights when she couldn't sleep. She knew if he died, she'd know it instantly, and that she didn't think she could bear. But that was what J.T. was telling her. The simple fact that he wanted to spend Kwanzaa with his family and then he was going to die, or die trying.

Teddi and J.T. sat at the kitchen table, eating. She'd decided to believe his story. She'd thought about it, and realized that J.T. had never lied to her. He'd never exactly told her that he was a computer salesman. He'd just let her have her assumptions.

"How's your leg?" she asked.

"It's just a shallow flesh wound. I'll be fine."

Teddi bit her lip, feeling guilty despite his reassurance. How could she have shot him? He was going to have to leave again, and resume the life of a fugitive. Would he be able to get around and elude his enemies? What if the wound got infected? She felt sick inside.

"You cut your finger," J.T. said, breaking into her thoughts.

She looked at her hand. She'd forgotten about the

cut. "The knife slipped when I was chopping vegetables," she said.

"You should put something on it."

Their conversation was hesitant and uneasy, like strangers none too comfortable with one another. Teddi remembered wistfully the time when words weren't necessary between them. Even their silences used to be full.

"Your fried chicken is so good. I used to dream about it," J.T. said. Then he chuckled. "Not saying your food was all I dreamed about you, but your food is mighty fine, among other things."

Teddi couldn't smile. She wasn't ready for easy banter yet. Her nerves were still too taut, her emotions barely in check.

"This chicken is my grandma's recipe," she said.

"She trained you well. How is your grandmother and the rest of the family?"

"They're fine. My parents have been very supportive. I don't know how I'd have made it through without them."

The shadow returned to J.T.'s face. "Nothing can erase the past, can it?"

"I've rebuilt a life here and it's pretty good. Sylvie and I will be all right with or without you."

Her words were cruel, but she had to make him walk away again without risking his life on a gamble with impossible odds. No matter how much losing him a second time hurt, at least she would know he was alive in the world with her.

J.T. winced and laid down the piece of chicken he was eating. "We were good together before all this happened. I need my family, Teddi, I need you."

Finally she looked at him, her eyes glistening. "I couldn't bear it if anything happened to you."

He reached for her hand. "I know how you feel. I

feel the same way about you and Sylvie. But nothing's going to happen to me, baby. I told you I was too good for that."

"I wonder how Sylvie's going to react when she sees you?" Teddi asked. She had to change the subject. The thought of the danger J.T. was in threatened to unravel her.

As J.T. opened his mouth to answer, she heard a key turning in the front door, followed by a babble of voices. Sylvie bounced into the kitchen, followed by Teddi's mother, grandmother, sisters, and assorted nieces and nephews. At the sight of her father, Sylvie froze. Conversation stopped and Teddi's family stared at J.T., speechless. Then, Sylvie's scream pierced the air as she launched herself at J.T.

The First Day of Kwanzaa

The Nguzo Saba is the principle of
UMOJA (Unity)
To strive for and maintain unity
in the family, community, nation,
and race.

Unity to be real must stand the severest strain without breaking.

—*Mahatma Gandhi*

Four

By and by when the morning comes, all the saints of
God are gathered home. We'll tell the story of how
we overcome, for we'll understand it better by and
by.

—*Traditional spiritual*

Tears and laughter mingled as J.T. cradled Sylvie in
his arms. The strained smile pasted on Teddi's face
almost hurt. Was it a dream come true to have the
only man she ever loved back and her family reunited,
or was it a nightmare? The love she had for J.T. had
been too strong to ever completely die, but his reappearance tied her insides into knots. She could hardly
stand it.

Teddi met her mother's eyes. Justine frowned, and
chewed her lower lip. God, what was she going to say
to her mother? Her parents had been pillars of
strength through the ordeal of losing J.T. She wasn't
sure how they would take his sudden reappearance.
She'd have to tell them everything. She owed them
that much.

"Daddy, come see my new room. You're staying now,

aren't you?" Sylvie didn't wait for an answer, and tugged at J.T.'s arm. Teddi wished she had the resilience and acceptance of a child. Sylvie took things at face value, simply happy and excited to have her daddy back. Teddi wished it was that easy for her.

"Yes, take your father and show him your room," Justine said. The rest of the family were unnaturally quiet, waiting and watching for some drama to erupt. Justine directed a frown at her children. "Teddi and I need to have a few words, please excuse us."

Her tone of voice brooked no hesitation, ifs, or buts, and everyone but Teddi cleared out to the living room.

"How dare he waltz back in here after what he's put you through," her mother said, the words exploding from deep within her.

"He had his reasons . . ."

"Damn his reasons, the man disappeared after embezzling money from his job, and setting your house on fire with two dead men inside. Do you realize that in addition to being a thief, he could be a murderer? Child, you call the police now and have them haul him away. You've been through enough with that man."

Justine sank into a kitchen chair, trembling with outrage. Teddi took her mother's hand in hers.

"Listen to me, Mom," she said. Justine shook her head, but was silent. "When I married J.T., he worked for the government. When he was in the military he was trained in intelligence and guerilla work, and after his tour of duty was up, he continued to work for the government, in a top secret capacity doing skilled and dangerous work." Teddi paused. "Do you understand?" she asked.

Justine looked skeptical, but nodded.

"When we got married, he stopped doing the dangerous work," Teddi continued. "But he still worked for the government. He says he was set up, Mom, and the only reason he fled was to ensure our safety. I believe him."

Justine raised an eyebrow. "You say he was doing secret agent stuff when you met him?"

"He was. You knew J.T., do you really think he is the type of man who would desert his family after embezzling money?" Teddi asked. "He left me enough money to buy this house with cash, without touching any insurance money."

"This house is just a drop in the bucket out of three million dollars," Justine answered.

"The company that he worked for, the one that accused him of stealing the money—they were a front for a covert government agency. There was never any company. And I always knew he didn't steal the money, Mama. I know my husband," Teddi said.

"I thought I knew J.T. Apparently, I didn't know him well enough. I was almost as stunned as you two years ago when he left you high and dry. Are his reasons good enough to make up for that, baby? Are you sure? It sounds like a load of . . ."

"I believe him," Teddi said again. "And I'm frightened. He says he's going to find the evidence that exonerates him, but I'm afraid he's just going to get himself killed."

Justine shook her head. "I know I didn't raise a fool, so you must have good reasons to allow J.T. back into your home. Just don't lose sight of what's really important in life; your daughter, your family, and the ones you love."

"That's what it's all about. Despite everything, I never stopped loving J.T."

Justine sighed. "When you married J.T. your father and I accepted him into our family as our son. Since you've let him back into your life, I don't suppose that's changed. He's disappointed us deeply, but I guess he's still family," she said, her voice reluctant.

Teddi saw her mother stare out the kitchen window into the deep gray blue Kansas night. Family was family, no matter what. These were the values Teddi had been raised with, and the values she knew her mother held dear to her heart. Her family would accept J.T. simply because Teddi still loved him. A lump grew in her throat as she thought about her blessing, her family. A blessing J.T. had never had. Then, Teddi heard Sylvie's high-pitched voice in the living room.

"We'd better go and join the others," she said to her mother.

Teddi and Justine left the room, and J.T. stood awkwardly along with the rest of the family. The silence thickened and grew uncomfortable until Teddi's father John cleared his throat. "J.T., we need to have a few words, come along to the den," he said.

J.T.'s heart sank. He'd almost rather face three armed men than Teddi's father right now. What could he say to him? The truth, he supposed, but the truth sounded so . . . crazy.

"Are you coming?" John asked, standing in the hallway. J.T. followed him, feeling like a small child on his way to the principal's office.

"Sit down," John said to him when they reached the den, while he closed the door firmly behind them. It wasn't until then that J.T. saw the flame of anger deep in his eyes. "I'm going to let you tell me why you have the audacity to show your face in my daughter's house before I call the police to cart you off to jail where you belong."

"I left for good reason, John," he said.

"It's hard to believe that any reason could be good enough for what you put Teddi through."

"I love Teddi and my child more than I love my own life. It tore out my heart to leave them. Believe me, my reasons for doing so are good enough."

"Three million dollars good, huh?" John asked.

J.T. rubbed his eyes with both hands. "I didn't take the money. I was set up," he said.

John's eyes narrowed as he watched J.T. "I'm no fool, young man," was all he said.

J.T. tried not to fidget under John's gaze. He remembered Teddi's father as the strong, silent type, never one to offer two words when one would do. He'd gotten up at 4:00 A.M. to go to his job at the packing plant for over forty years. He was a Deacon at the Baptist church where he'd been a member all his life. And J.T. knew nothing was more important to John than his family and his home, and his daughter Teddi. John would have a hard time forgiving the pain he'd caused his daughter. As hard a time as J.T. was having forgiving himself. At that moment, he'd have given anything for his story to sound more—plausible.

"The men that wanted to kill me planned to kill Teddi and Sylvie in front of me to make me talk," he said. "They wanted me to give them information that I didn't have. Information that I still don't have." J.T. studied his hands. "I killed them both. They were the bodies pulled from the house when it burned."

He continued looking at his hands until John shifted in his seat. "Why did people want to kill you?" John asked. "Were you involved in a drug organization?"

J.T. shot a glance at him. "No, the organization I was involved in is far more powerful and dangerous. I was an undercover agent for the government."

* * *

When Teddi walked into the living room with Justine following, she saw J.T. sitting in one recliner holding Sylvie in his lap. Her father was in the other recliner. Her brother Ronnie and his wife Stacy sat on the couch looking concerned, with their children at their feet playing some game. Her sister Eddie lay on the floor reading *Essence* magazine.

J.T. eased Sylvie off his lap, stood, and approached Justine. He kissed her cheek, and murmured something in her ear, but Justine didn't relax.

"I owe you all an explanation," he said, breaking the uneasy silence. "I wanted more than anything in the world to rejoin my family for Kwanzaa. I love them and miss them, but I had to leave to ensure their safety."

Justine crossed to the sofa and sat, not quite able to meet his eyes. J.T. returned to the recliner and picked up Sylvie, who snuggled against him.

"I have the blood of many men on my hands," he bit his lip and stared at his hands. Teddi heard her family drawing in a collective intake of breath.

"Blood not shed only in defense of myself or my family, but senseless blood poured out at the behest of a government whose purposes and principles I became disillusioned with long ago. Men who had mothers and lovers . . . men like me," J.T. continued.

He paused, and Sylvie reached up and touched his face. He gazed at his daughter, seemingly drawing strength from the sight of her face. "When I met Teddi, I felt that God had absolved me of my crimes, but now I'm not sure. Blood follows me."

His words held the family spellbound. Sylvie dozed while he talked, secure in her daddy's arms, lulled by the sound of his voice. J.T. told of his military training and his subsequent career. He talked about what had caused him to break his vow never to take a life again. He told about the two years he spent on the run as a fugitive. He left nothing out, and when he finished talking, his face was taut and drawn.

Tears gathered in Teddi's eyes. J.T. was not a talker or a confider. She alone knew how hard this was for him.

Her family was a tableau, unmoving and still. Her father sat in the recliner, staring at some point far away. Ronnie and his family were grouped together on the sofa. Eddie lay on a floor pillow, her eyes never moving once from J.T.'s face. Justine was in a chair on one side of the Kwanzaa table, her features immobile. Teddi sat in the chair on the other side of the table. She stroked a sculpture from The Gambia, like she could draw strength from the wood.

"I want to ask all of you for a gift," J.T. said. "I'm asking for silence. Let me spend Kwanzaa with my family in peace and safety, then I will go and ensure justice is done. I won't return until I'm a free man. If it's discovered that I'm here by the authorities, I have to go. Please grant me this Kwanzaa season."

Ronnie extended his hand. "Welcome back to the family, man."

Eddie looked at Teddi. "Girl, why do you get all the excitement in your life? It's not fair." Teddi rolled her eyes. Her sister had to be kidding.

Everyone looked toward John. Teddi's father looked down, considering. "I always felt there had to be more than appeared on the surface of what happened two years ago," he said, his words slow.

Then his eyes pierced J.T. "I try to leave it to God to judge. My gut instincts tell me you're a man of honor, and I feel you love my daughter."

He nodded his head, as if finally coming to a decision, and looked toward his wife. Justine moved by his side, lending her support and approval.

"You have our silence," she said. "We're family, and family sticks together. No matter what."

Five

For one lost, all lost—the chain that held them would save all or none.

—Toni Morrison

After the family left, Teddi had bathed Sylvie and now J.T. was reading her a bedtime story. Teddi finished arranging the fruits and vegetables on the Kwanzaa table, then stood back to survey her handiwork. Everything was ready for tomorrow. Red, black, and green streamers graced the room, and the flag faced the east.

Every year Teddi hung the Pan-African flag for the Kwanzaa holiday. She faced the flag east, toward the Motherland. The flag was three simple horizontal stripes, red at the top representing blood shed in the struggle for freedom and liberation. The black stripe in the middle symbolized the color of the people, and at the bottom, the green of the land.

The dining room table was covered with kente cloth with a sculpture of animals native to Africa serving as the centerpiece. Everything was ready except the cooking. On the first day of Kwanzaa, Teddi always prepared a meal from West Africa, the land of her ancestors. Food is important to any holiday, and for each of the seven days, Teddi made a meal reflecting the roots and origins of black people. She cooked dishes not only from Africa, but from the new lands where the children of Africa had been scattered: Traditional soul food, Caribbean dishes, and South American and Brazilian food. She'd need to prepare the ginger beer tonight, because it needed to sit out overnight.

Also on the first day of Kwanzaa, Teddi always invited close friends, people who had stood in as her and J.T.'s extended family when she lived back East. This year her real extended family was coming, and sharing the experience with them excited her. She hoped that the celebration of their common roots, ancestors, and culture meant as much to her family as it had come to mean to her.

Traditions were important to Teddi, and she took care in creating them. Kwanzaa lent itself beautifully to the creation of individual family traditions. It was a new, vibrant holiday, growing and changing to reflect the people. The rituals and trappings of Kwanzaa were a mere skeleton to be fleshed out and made ones's own, by each family and each community.

She turned toward the kitchen and soon was chopping fresh ginger, the pungent fragrance bringing tears to her eyes. The warm glow of her family's love and support still warmed her. They'd all been crazy about J.T. and almost as shocked and devastated by his defection as she'd been.

J.T. entered the kitchen and stood close behind her. "She's asleep," he said. He put his arms around her and pulled her against his warm body. His musky male scent enveloped her. Teddi laid down the knife against the cutting board and closed her eyes.

Her problem was that she understood her mother's

hesitation in accepting and trusting J.T. too well. There was a hidden corner inside that raged at him and wondered if he'd suffered a fraction of the pain he'd caused her to feel.

Another part of her wanted to take him to bed. Right now, that was the part that was winning. Teddi relaxed, leaning back against J.T., melting into his body. Yes, this was what she wanted, what she craved; J.T.'s hard body against hers. She'd been so lonely.

"Your family is wonderful. You don't know what it means to me to be able to spend this time with you," he said, his voice low in her ear, the warm moisture of his whisper caressing her cheek.

"J.T.—" Teddi started to say, her voice strangled.

"Shhh, you've been through enough today. Go to bed and rest up for all that cooking I know you're planning to do tomorrow. We'll talk some more than."

Talking wasn't what Teddi had on her mind.

"I'll sleep in the guest bedroom," J.T. added.

He pulled away from her and filled the teapot with water. Conversation petered away, and awkwardness filled the room. We're like strangers, Teddi thought. Two years apart changed then both. "J.T.?" she asked. He looked up.

"The time you were gone . . . Where did you live? What did you do?"

J.T. reached for a mug and dropped a teabag into it before he answered. He left the mug on the stove until the water boiled and sat at the table.

"I lived in third-rate motels. I carried everything I owned in a duffle bag. I spent my time alone. I watched more TV in the past two years than I watched in my lifetime before. I stayed on the move, from city to city and state to state. I left you half of the savings I squirreled away, I carried the other half and paid cash for everything. I ate, I slept, I existed. And I missed my family."

"I'm sorry, J.T. Sorry for both of us," she said.

The teapot whistled. "So am I, baby," he said. He poured the boiling water into the mug. "I'm going to lie down and read a little," he paused, like there was something else he wanted to say. "Good night, Teddi," was all he said.

The words fell in the room like rocks and lay there. She bit her lip and stared at his back as he exited. There was so much they still had to talk about. She picked up the knife and started to chop the ginger. Would the losing, the needing, the wanting ever end? J.T.'s reappearance had opened her wound afresh. Two years had been barely enough to form a scab. And all the explanations in the world couldn't erase the pain.

Teddi blamed the ginger for the tears that leaked down her cheeks. Tomorrow was the first day of Kwanzaa, Umosa, and it appeared as if God had already worked a miracle in her life, giving her husband back to her. She shouldn't live in the past or for the future. The present was all that existed, and she should enjoy what it had to offer, moment by moment. She refused to worry any longer, or dwell on her anger or fear. What she would do was to pray for another miracle.

J.T. sat up against the headboard of the guestroom bed, the words of the book he was trying to read blurring into an abstract of black on white. He was a guest in his wife's house. He'd missed Teddi and Sylvie so much, he'd passed the point where he could willfully do without them any longer. His weakness might put the ones he loved most in the world in danger. What was he thinking of?

His stomach knotted. Out there, people wanted to

kill him. They'd stop at nothing to trap and hunt him down, even if it meant using what he loved most. He'd not been forgotten in the two years he'd been gone. He was a wild card, a variable that somehow could trip up someone's game plan.

He rubbed the place where he'd cleaned and bandaged the wound in his thigh. He was mighty lucky the bullet had barely grazed his flesh. He still couldn't get over that Teddi had actually shot him. Not that he didn't deserve it, even though leaving her had been the hardest thing he'd ever done in his life . . . until he discovered that staying away was even harder. Staying out of her bed tonight, pain and all, right now was hardest of all.

Teddi was crisp and no-nonsense through the day, but he remembered oh, so well, how she melted into sweet, soft passion in his arms. She'd never bored him like so many other women did. With her there was always something new, some undiscovered facet of her to learn. They simply fit each other like well worn jeans. It wasn't fair that their life had been derailed so suddenly and completely.

He wanted to rage and to strike out, but his enemies were nameless, their motives unknown. What was it that Paul had uncovered? He'd left no clues, and the grave told no tales. J.T. had spent two long years searching, never coming closer than a tantalizing waft of the truth.

Despite his brave talk to Teddi, he hadn't found any leads to solve the mystery, and he tasted bitter despair. This was his last goodbye to his family. He wouldn't continue living in limbo, in fear for his family. After Kwanzaa, he was going out to do or die.

Odors of cooking started to fill the house. J.T. smiled to himself. It was after eight, but Teddi would always clean or cook when she had something on her mind. She seemed more fragile somehow, and he glimpsed the lingering echo of hurt in her eyes that had once held only expectation and contentment. He hated the fact that he'd wounded her, and vowed to give her space and time.

He would wait to hold his wife in his arms again. The load he carried on his heart lightened, he was home again. For the first time in two long years he drifted into untroubled sleep.

Her body was draped in white diaphanous gauze, accentuating moonlit dark satin skin and the shadowed womanly crevices of her body. With one smooth motion she dropped the straps and the gown fell to the floor like forgotten cobwebs.

J.T.'s mouth dried as his body responded to her with a rush of heat. How often had he dreamed this? But this was no dream. His wife was real, and she had come to him.

Then she was in his arms and he could have wept with the reality of it all. She was all he ever wanted and needed. His hands and lips moved of themselves, worshipping at the temple of her body, touching, tasting, and rediscovering the full African lushness, the womanly musk of her passion. He ran his hand down the curve of her back, over the swell of her belly, his fingers, his soul delighting in the velvety texture of her skin.

A whimper emerged from deep within, her eyes dark, bottomless pools.

"How can I live without you?" he murmured, his words more a plea than a question. He was drowning with want, his need becoming keen as a knife's edge. Ancient rhythms captured him, and took them both over.

He was a part of her, and when they become one, he took her with him to the edge of heaven, and they plummeted to completion connected, two hearts, two souls melded.

Returning to earth, their breaths slowing, not yet ready to move apart, Teddi traced the outline of his lips. "We can't live without each other. It's not how our world is meant to be."

J.T. kissed her finger. He didn't want to think about how many things in the world existed that weren't meant to be. He didn't want to think about anything outside of this magical moment, finally reunited with the woman he loved. He didn't want to stop.

Then, again, not separating, two halves rejoined, they made the slow, honeyed languid love that comes only with familiarity. He knew where and how to touch her. Long ago, he'd learned her rhythms, when she liked it slow and easy, when she wanted it hard and driving. He knew how to interpret her sounds of passion. Now, he existed only to please her, his true love.

He couldn't make up for two years of lovemaking missed, but he could try. He brought her to the peak of passion again and again, until she begged for mercy, until she begged for more. Until he became lost in her passion himself, until reason left him and instinct took over.

Hours later, Teddi lay across his chest, their hearts beating as one. Time had rushed on without them, and the pink dawn peeked through the windows from the eastern sky.

"I can't let you go again," she whispered.

J.T.'s heart started a slow, heavy thud in his chest. He knew she'd have to.

"Don't leave me again, J.T. We're a family, and we have to face whatever we have to face, united," Teddi said.

"I can't take the risk. Protecting my family comes first."

"No," she answered back, her voice shaking with intensity.

"I had to make the hard decisions, and stand by them."

He'd have to make them again. He could almost feel Teddi withdraw emotionally. He gathered her close to him.

"What's out there isn't going to ruin this time with you, with my family. Harambee, my love."

Teddi clutched him to her fiercely like she'd never let him go. "Harambee," she answered.

Six

When spiderwebs unite, they can tie up a lion.
                                        —*Ethiopian proverb*

Teddi chopped and mashed, boiled and fried, allowing the routines of the kitchen to carry her. She hummed as she worked, her mind working as fast and furious as her hands.

Did it even matter that there was even the glimmer of doubt that J.T. stole three million dollars and then abandoned her for two years? Did it make the slightest difference that there was the faintest possibility that he waltzed into this house, lying like a rug with some cockamamy story about secret agents and government conspiracies?

As long as he made good love, it was all good, right? And if nothing else, he did make good love. The knife slipped and dug into her thumb. At this rate her hands were going to be a mass of cuts. She was a little more anxious than usual. The cooking was not soothing her as well as she first supposed.

The doorbell interrupted her thoughts. Eddie's beautiful face peeked through the glass pane. "Hurry up and let me in, it's cold out here," she said. Eddie blew in with a gust of frosty wind. "I see your hubby is making himself useful, but Lord, couldn't that wait until spring?"

J.T. was outside on a ladder fixing a drooping gutter. Teddi shrugged. "I think he wanted to get out. Here, you can make yourself useful and help me dice these onions."

"I'd almost forgotten how godforsaken boring this town is. I had to get out of the house," Eddie said. "Is all you ever do, cook?"

"Around Kwanzaa, it seems like that. But I like to cook."

"Where's Sylvie?" Eddie asked.

"In the den watching her favorite video for the umpteenth time," Teddi answered, getting out another knife for her sister.

They'd always grated on each other's nerves, she and Eddie. They were too close and yet altogether different. Maybe it started with their names. Teddi's full name was Theodosina, and if that wasn't bad enough, two years later their mother had named the new baby Edwina. Teddi and Eddie, they'd struggled against one another ever since Eddie had usurped Teddi's coveted place in the family as the youngest child. And Eddie seemed to have never gotten over the resentment of being the recipient of Teddi hand-me-downs, toys, clothes, and later boyfriends.

They'd gloried in the contrast between them, they were almost exact opposites in looks and personality. Teddi's looks were quiet, all tailored class, striking rather than beautiful.

Eddie was outrageously beautiful, with cinnamon skin and long black hair. She made sure her beauty wasn't the only outrageous thing about her. She was flamboyant and outspoken, verging on brash with movie-star style. She'd barely turned eighteen when she'd left Kansas far behind and took off for the opposite coast from her sister.

The years passed and their lives still continued to contrast. Teddi was thirty-four now, with the history of being a stay-at-home mom in a solid marriage with a home in the suburbs, and all the trappings of the American dream behind her. Eddie was thirty-two, with two marriages, both to actors, behind her. She sold pricey real estate, did very well financially, and swore she'd never leave L.A.

Emotionally, Teddi worried about her. Eddie always had a man hovering around her, but as they both grew older, Teddi had glimpsed flashes of loneliness. When Eddie had watched her nieces and nephews open their presents yesterday morning, she'd spoken almost wistfully of having a child. Teddi thought her sister's biological clock must be ticking louder. She wished Eddie would find the right man to settle down with.

Eddie took a few halfhearted swipes at an onion before she laid the knife down. "My eyes are starting to burn. I hate cutting onions. I always buy those precut frozen kind," she said. She glanced around at the scale of Teddi's preparations for the celebration. "You're really going all out. I've barely recovered from Christmas. You really go for this ethnic stuff, don't you?"

"I think Kwanzaa is good for my family. It really renews our spirit, and we all need to take more pride in our roots."

"Whatever," Eddie said with a wave of a perfectly manicured hand. "Girl, the drama in your life now. Long-lost husband turning up with tales of conspiracy, blood, and gore. Great stuff. It would make a good movie."

"Watching it on the big screen and living it are two different things. I'd do anything for all this drama to

go away, and things to be like they were before he left."
Teddi couldn't control the quaver of her voice and the
expression on Eddie's face sobered.

"I'm sorry, I don't mean to make light of your situation. What are you going to do? There's a warrant out
for his arrest. What if the police take him in?"

"I don't want to think about it anymore, Eddie. I just
have to live by the moment, and right now he's back
here with us, and that makes me happy."

Uncharacteristically, Eddie reached out to touch
Teddi's hand. "Love can be a mean dog, sis," she said.

"That it can, Eddie, that it can."

Eddie soon left to drive to Topeka to do some shopping. Teddi had fed Sylvie earlier, and helped her with
the tale she was going to recite during the festivities
tonight. Sylvie had begged to go and play with her cousins. Teddi hesitated, then let her go, reminding her that
her father's presence in the house was only to be shared
with family. J.T. was outside messing with the house,
and Teddi was alone with her thoughts again.

She and J.T. were fasting during the daylight hours
of Kwanzaa as had been their custom. Well, she had to
taste the dishes she was preparing to get the seasoning
right, but surely that didn't count. She wandered into
the living room, and noticed the Bible sitting open on
her desk. J.T. must have been reading the Bible, and a
smidgen of fear touched her heart. Was he preparing
to meet his maker? No, she reassured herself, the days
of Kwanzaa were a time for cleansing, reflection, prayer,
and meditation.

She sat down in front of the Bible and let the timeless
beauty of the words wash over her. It must have been
an hour later when she heard the front door slam shut
and she started, looking up for the first time from the

Bible stories that had caught and held her. J.T. entered the room blowing on his hands.

"Mighty cold out there," he said. "I got that gutter fixed."

Teddi smiled at him, her anger and confusion finally dissipating to the quiet warmth they used to share.

She could close her eyes and imagine that it was five years ago, the atmosphere of their home as comfortable and easy as a pair of well-loved slippers. Sylvie was a toddler, and they all had spent the first day of Kwanzaa in companionable togetherness, their intimacy unquestioned, with no hint of the darkness that would cloud their future.

"Good, baby. I'm happy you fixed the gutter," Teddi heard herself saying. "It's all good."

Teddi patted her headwrap as she opened the door to let her family in. She'd made matching gowns of African fabric for herself and Sylvie. The unaccustomed clothing suited her. The house soon filled with her parents, aunts, uncles, cousins, nieces and nephews, brothers and sisters. The babble of conversation and the laughter and shrieks of children filled the air along with the soft scent of the incense.

Teddi and J.T. opted to keep it simple this year. She'd been to Kwanzaa celebrations with drums, and plenty of ceremonial trappings, but her family was a simple lot. Eyes were already lingering on the mouth-watering West African buffet she had set out. Teddi knew her folks and was pleased the ceremony would be short.

"Habari gani?" J.T. asked the people gathered. He was clad simply in blue jeans and a sweater, and Teddi's heart overflowed as she gazed at him. She couldn't keep her joy in at having her family reunited.

"Umoja," Teddi and Sylvie chorused in unison.

"Umoja," some of her family chimed in belatedly.

"Let's eat," Uncle Kelly grumbled and Teddi suppressed a smile.

"I'd kick my husband's butt if he had the nerve to show back up after leaving me high and dry." Teddi heard Aunt Mae whisper to her mother in a stage whisper.

"She shot him," her mother answered.

Teddi grinned wryly to herself. Her mother sure did know how to shut folks up.

J.T. picked up the kikombe cha umoja, the unity cup, in preparation for the libation, or tambiko, the African custom of pouring a small amount of one's drink on the ground for the honor and respect of the ancestors.

"In remembrance of our ancestors who lived the Nguzo Saba of umoja, unity, we celebrate the spirit of all those who have gone on before. We celebrate Martin Luther King, Jr., who united our people to stand up for a common cause."

Uncle Kelly and Aunt Jenna nodded at the mention of Martin Luther King, Jr.

"We honor the Motherland, Africa," J.T. continued. "We honor our ancestors who struggled to preserve their culture and unity in the face of insurmountable odds. We honor our elders, for the wisdom and experience they give us. We honor our young, the hope for our future. We remember Umoja the principle of Unity, which binds us together and makes us strong. And above all we honor our God, the Creator, who has granted life and love to all people of the earth."

J.T. took the cup and poured a bit of water on a platter he'd placed on the floor. Then, he took a sip from the cup and passed it to Teddi who stood next to him. "To symbolize our unity," he said.

The cup went around the room in reverent silence. Finally the cup returned to J.T.

"Sylvie," he said. Teddi lit a taper and handed it to her daughter. Sylvie lit the black candle in the center of the kinara.

"For unity," she said in her high little girl's voice. A smile broke over J.T.'s face that lit up his handsome features.

"Let's eat," he said. And nobody needed to be urged a second time.

When everyone had eaten their fill, Teddi asked her sister to put some soft jazz on the CD and she stood by the Kwanzaa table.

"Sylvie is going to tell a story reflecting the Nguzo Saba of this day. She's going to tell a story about unity," she announced. Conversation ceased and the room became quiet. She took her daughter's hand and drew her to the chair she'd placed by the Kwanzaa table. Sylvie cleared her throat and began.

"It was December 1955 in Montgomery, Alabama," Sylvie said. "African-American people had to enter the bus and pay their fee by the front door, then get off the bus and enter again by the back door.

"They had to sit at the back of the bus, while the white people sat in the front. Rosa Parks had just finished a hard day at work and was sitting in the middle section of the bus when a white person got on the bus.

"The front of the bus was filled, and the bus driver told Rosa to get up and stand in the back so the white man could sit in the middle. Rosa said no. The bus driver called the police and they put her into jail.

"Martin Luther King, Jr., a Montgomery minister, became involved in organizing a boycott of the bus company. That means nobody was to ride the buses anymore. The entire African-American community in that city united together so they wouldn't have to ride

the bus. They walked, they shared rides, they rode bi-
cycles and horses—anything but get on the bus.

"But the bus company wouldn't give in. Finally in
November 1956, the Supreme Court said that the bus
company was wrong. Segregation ended that day, the
name of Martin Luther King, Jr., was heard throughout
the nation. And all because of the will and unity of
African-American people in one small city."

Sylvie took a deep breath at the end of her story, and
looked up at her mother. "I'm done," she said. The
room burst into applause.

"Harambee means lets pull together," Teddi said,
once the applause died. "Pull together and there is
nothing we can't accomplish and no fight we can't win."

"Harambee," J.T. echoed. Their eyes met, and
Teddi's heart leapt. He was telling her that he wasn't
going anywhere. They would stay united as a family, and
as a family, they would overcome anything.

The Second Day of Kwanzaa

The Nguzo Saba is the principle of
KUJICHAGULIA (Self-determination)
To define ourselves, create for ourselves,
speak for ourselves instead of being defined,
named, created for and spoken for by others.

i found god in myself & i loved her/i loved her
fiercely

—*Ntozake Shange*

Seven

In the midst of our own crisis, our own life problems,
the power of our deliverance is in our own power in
our own possession.
    —*C. L. Franklin, "The Moses and the Red Sea." 1957.*

The morning sun had always uplifted Teddi's spirit,
but now she craved the dark—the deep quiet night time
when her body and soul entangled with J.T.'s, when the
world receded and it was just her and the man she loved.

When he entered her and they became one, their ec-
stasy soaring, they were joined at the heart, soul mates
never meant to be separated. The stubble of his beard
abraded her tender skin, and her body trembled under
the gentle strength of his love. Perfection was here and
now, and Teddi wanted time to stop and now to be always.

Damp and spent, they rested, still joined, unwilling
to part even in sleep. Teddi woke first, J.T.'s leg thrown
over her body, entrapping her, his arms possessively
drawing her close. She used to always awake with a
prayer of thankfulness. In addition to her life, health,
and her daughter, she was overwhelmingly thankful for
being granted such a rare love. In the back of her mind

dwelled the fear that she'd done something wrong to have it snatched away so abruptly. Was it restored now only to tease her? To remind of her what she had to lose again?

No, she was not going to lose this, she decided. She wasn't going to let J.T. waltz out of her life again with his male sense of overprotection. They were going to fight this thing together. It was her life and her right. These people, this conspiracy J.T. talked about, had stolen two years of their lives already, and she was not going to let it steal a second more.

Teddi slid away from J.T. to go to the bathroom, and when she returned, he was awake.

"Habari gani?" he asked, a look of contentment on his face as Teddi snuggled back into his arms. "Kujichagulia," she replied. "And coincidentally, self-determination is what we need to talk about."

J.T. raised an eyebrow.

"I'm not going to allow these people to control . . . no, to destroy our lives."

"I told you that after Kwanzaa, I was going to set everything straight," he said.

"Jethro Temple Henderson, we are going to set things straight together."

J.T. winced at hearing his full name. He was no more a Jethro than she was a Theodosina.

"We have to stop letting this thing control our destiny. We've got to find a way to fight together," she continued.

A shadow crossed his face. "There would be no point in living if I allowed anything to happen to you and Sylvie."

"There's no point in living without you, and I won't do it. Right is right, and we have God on our side. When I found out you were still alive, that you had left me and Sylvie, when they told me that you embezzled three million dollars from the company you worked for, and possibly killed two men, I wanted to die. If it wasn't for Sylvie, I might have. Then I got mad."

"I see that you stayed mad," J.T. said wryly, rubbing his injured thigh.

"I guess I did. I just couldn't believe that you'd walk out on me after all we had together. I never even opened the second letter you sent me later."

"What second letter?" he asked. "I only wrote you one letter to say goodbye. Right after I left New York I went to Washington, D.C., frantically trying to find out what was happening. Then I knew better to stay in contact with you, it would have been too tempting, and I had to stay away no matter what. I sent no second letter."

"I assumed this letter I received a few weeks after you left was from you. It was obviously a handwritten, personal letter addressed to me with no return address and a New York City postmark. Hold on, I kept it. Someday when the hurt eased, and I could deal with what you had to say, I planned to read it."

J.T. shifted and looked at her intently.

Getting up, she pulled her robe on, and went to the file cabinet by her desk. She rummaged through the papers, and returned to find J.T. sitting on the edge of the bed, leaning forward.

"Here it is," she exclaimed, thrusting the letter at J.T.

He tore it open and read it quickly. "It's from Paul," he said, sucking in a breath through his teeth. "I think it's the key we need to get out of this mess."

The morning sun was high in the sky and it had snowed during the night. The yard was clothed in fresh, clean white, glittering like diamonds. Now, like the new fallen snow, she and J.T. had a chance at a fresh start. His old friend Paul had left him a way out from beyond the grave. They simply had to figure out a way to take advantage of it.

The first thing that fell out of the envelope when J.T. opened it was a note someone scratched, saying Paul told them to send the letter if they didn't hear from him in a month.

"Paul says he was afraid," J.T. said, reading the letter.

"He obviously had reason to be," Teddi said. She heard the sound of the television from the den. Sylvie was up. Her daughter could fix herself a bowl of cereal if she was hungry, Teddi wasn't about to move from the warmth of her bed and J.T.'s revelations.

"He wasn't afraid enough," J.T. answered. "It says he's secreted concrete evidence for me to retrieve and go public with if anything happens to him.

"Thank you, God," Teddi said, with feeling.

"Not so soon. There's no way I can get close. The information is backed up as an obscure inventory file on the computer's mainframe. I've got to be there to find and download it. They have good security in place.

"There's got to be a way, we only have to discover it," Teddi said.

He nodded and pulled her to him. "There's always a way." He gazed at her face a long minute and smoothed her hair back with a gentle movement.

"God knows I don't want to leave you," he murmured, and touched his lips to hers.

The kiss was tender at first. He tasted her, his hunger growing, deepening, and soon their bodies strained to join once again. Urgent and breathless, they both soared to the heavens along with the climb of the morning sun.

* * *

"I wish you'd stop worrying. We decided to trust that boy's word, and that's that," John said.

Justine shook her head. "Teddi was so hurt when J.T. left. She's made a life for herself here. I'd hate to see her hurt again."

"It's her life, Justine. You can't live it for her. All we can do is to be there when she needs us." John folded the paper and stood up, stretching. "I'm going to organize those kitchen cabinets of yours. I don't see how you function in that kitchen, with everything thrown hither and thither like that." He left the room muttering.

Justine opened her mouth to say something, then closed it. Lord, give her strength. If she let John know what was on her mind, the blast might rock the foundations of their home. Forty years of marriage, through the good and the bad, and she couldn't remember when she wanted to do him in more than she wanted it right now. Slow poison, something that wouldn't be detected. She'd collect the insurance money and retire in the Virgin Islands.

Now that was a thought. And to think she'd looked forward to John's retirement. They even threw him a party when he'd gotten home from his last day at the packing plant. That was six months ago, and he was driving her insane. She was going raving bonkers and it was no longer a laughing matter.

He'd started with the garage, and that was fine. Then he rearranged everything in the storage shed out back, and that was good. She'd gotten a little uneasy when he spent three hundred dollars on plastic storage boxes and rearranged the whole basement. But that was all right, the basement looked better than it had in years.

Still, she asked him about his plans for his retirement. John looked at her blankly and said, "Honey, I'm going to take a well-deserved rest." She nodded then, a smile forming that quickly faded when he added, "I plan to help you out around the house, also. I see a lot of things that need a little more order around here."

He'd been following her around ever since. Do it like this, he'd say, do it like that. She could hardly find a thing without asking him anymore. May the Lord have mercy on her soul, but the thought of divorce crossed her mind. She needed to pray about it, and then she'd sit down and talk to John. Everything would be just fine. Because it sure couldn't get much worse.

"But I don't want to go," Sylvie complained. "I want to stay here with Daddy.

"Daddy's busy with the computer right now. Don't you want to go with me to say goodbye to your cousins?"

"Not really, I've seen them enough," Sylvie grumbled, but soon subsided with a look from Teddi.

At Teddi's parents' home, amid the hubbub of loading up the car with the gifts, fetching forgotten things, and kisses and hugs goodbye, she was surprised to see Eddie there. Eddie was supposed to leave with Ronnie to catch a plane back to L.A.

"What's up, sis? I thought you were going with Ronnie to KCI airport?" Teddi asked.

Eddie gave her a lazy smile and thrust her hands into the pockets of her parka. "I couldn't resist staying a few days longer. You finally got some drama in your life, and I wanted to stick around and see what happens."

Teddi grimaced. She'd always been the stable, predictable one until two years ago when her life crashed down around her. Until then, the crisis and drama always belonged to Eddie. Her sister was vicariously enjoying her experience. Well, she wished Eddie could have it.

"Whatever," Teddi said and shrugged.

"Mama, I want to go back home to Daddy," Sylvie said.

"I'll go with you. I want to see what you have cooking anyway," Eddie said.

"When you walk into my kitchen, you realize you're going to have to do some cooking," Teddi warned.

"Just don't make me cut up any onions," Eddie said.

Teddi grinned at her sister. Despite her love for predictability, and all their differences, she knew she could trust her sister, and Eddie's shoulder was always available to lean on if needed. Teddi was glad she was staying a few more days.

They'd no sooner gotten in the door and laid down their coats when the doorbell rang. She opened the door to the smiling face of her mailman, holding out a package for her.

"Cold weather, huh?" he said.

Teddi nodded. "We're supposed to get a warm spell next week," she offered.

"I saw the gentleman working on your gutters the other day. I thought it was a mighty cold day for outside work. He one of your relations from out of town?"

Teddi's smile grew frosty. "No," she said.

"I heard you used to be married. Tough, huh, my daughter tells me how hard it is to find a good husband."

Wilkins was unbelievably nosy, but usually harmless. But now, this was a little much to take. "Thanks for the package, have a happy new year," Teddi said, retreating, closing the door.

"You, too," Wilkins called.

This morning her mother had told her that some people in town were making comments about "the man she moved in." There was no way she could keep J.T.'s presence a secret in such a small town. She'd have to think of a way to explain him if she decided to bother. She could care less about her reputation.

She worried about the few people who knew her history. What if they put it together and figured out J.T. was her husband? What if someone turned him in? Once the police had him, his whereabouts would be revealed, and if the people after him were as serious as J.T. seemed to believe and their memories as long, they could be in terrible danger.

"That man had his nerve, didn't he?" Eddie said, her hand on her hip.

"I'm getting scared. Don't they have those most wanted posters at the post office? What if he suspects something?" Teddi asked.

"If he doesn't suspect what a fool he is by now, he's not going to suspect a thing. Don't worry so much. Our local police are busy gorging themselves on free donuts and taking naps in their squad cars. Nothing ever happens in this town."

"That's precisely why I'm worried. Something just has, and people don't have anything else to talk about."

"Ain't that the truth," Eddie said, growing bored with the subject. "What do you have to eat?" she asked.

Eight

We will either find a way or make one.

—*Hannibal*

Teddi fed Sylvie and Eddie and tried to ignore the grumbling of her stomach. On the second day of Kwanzaa, Teddi usually didn't plan to have guests. She liked to cook a traditional African-American meal of their favorites for dinner, and use the day to bond as a nuclear family, and to evaluate and determine the family's direction. She was marinating one of J.T.'s favorite meals, smothered pork chops. She wished he would be around long enough so she could get some good solid meat on his bones.

Teddi realized what she'd just thought and rubbed her sleeve over her eyes. *Be around long enough.* She prayed they could make it so. She also didn't dwell on the relief she felt at seeing the concrete evidence that J.T. was telling the truth, the letter from Paul. Of course, she believed him, but . . . it made a difference, that's all.

Once she would have trusted J.T. if he told her the sky was red and the moon resided in the ocean. But that was before her world had cracked its foundations, spilling everything she once believed in the streets for everyone to see that she'd lived a lie.

J.T. was working on the computer. He'd been at it most of the morning, except he had stopped for a while to play with Sylvie. She wanted to talk, but the intense look on his face didn't invite interruption.

She was a wreck, a bundle of raw nerve endings. J.T. had brought a cloud of fear with him, thick and suffocating. The rhymes and reasons were now known, and the enemy was more than she'd ever imagined. They had to find a way out. Soon.

She wondered what they could do to increase their security and ensure their safety until they decided what they were going to do. Sylvie was out playing in the snow with the neighborhood children. Teddi hadn't wanted to let her go out alone, but the excitement in Sylvie's deep brown eyes at the thought of playing in the snow persuaded her. She couldn't keep her daughter closed up in the house, however much she wanted to.

Teddi jumped as J.T. quietly approached her from behind and wrapped his arms around her waist. He nuzzled her neck.

"Nervous?" he asked.

Teddi nodded. "People are asking questions about you. I don't know what to say to them, I'm so afraid . . ." Teddi paused with a sharp intake of breath as J.T. pulled her around to him. He kissed her lips and trailed tiny kisses down the side of her neck, inhaling the scent of her.

"Tell them I'm your cousin from out of town. By marriage."

"Seriously, J.T."

J.T. lifted his head and looked at her. "I am serious. And I'm afraid, too. I've been trying to figure out a way to get into the NIA's mainframe all day. I can't. I have to go there."

"You're not going in," Teddi said.

"It's the only way, baby."

"It's not the only way." She paused. "I want to go in for you."

J.T.'s body stiffened and he pulled away. "That's out of the question," he said, his voice low and dangerous.

"You agreed we're in this together. I don't see any other options. They'll recognize you instantly. At least I have a chance to pull it off."

"Conversation is closed, Teddi. I'm going in right after Kwanzaa to retrieve the file Paul left, and that's final." His expression softened as he read the worried, almost distraught look on Teddi's face. "It'll be all right, baby, you'll see. Remember you're the one who said we have God on our side."

Teddi glanced up at him from underneath her lashes. Men were so stubborn. Women sometimes needed to quietly take matters into their own hands.

"John, we need to talk," Justine said. They were alone at the table. Eddie was out, and she'd prepared his favorite pot roast for lunch. She was going to tell him it wasn't working. The house was her domain, and he needed to find something else constructive to do with his retirement other than drive her crazy.

John smiled at her. "Yes, we do need to talk," he said. He pulled out a piece of paper from his pocket.

"What's that?" she asked.

"Your schedule. Now that I'm home, I notice that you could get more done with wiser use of your time." He shoved the paper at her. She didn't touch it.

"I know it's hard sticking to a schedule at first, but

it'll pay off . . ." John's voice trailed away as he gazed at the look on her face. "Is anything wrong?" he asked.

"I don't need a schedule," Justine replied, carefully keeping her voice even and modulated.

His face fell. "I worked hard on it, I wish you would try it out."

She picked up the piece of paper and raised an eyebrow as she read it. She'd love to tell him where he could stick his schedule. Maybe he was kidding. She looked at him closely. Her husband sat there looking serious and completely earnest. He honestly had no clue. She laid the schedule down.

"John, you being around the house all day isn't working for either of us," she said.

"You're saying you don't want me around?" he asked, looking hurt. She felt as if she'd kicked a puppy. One of those annoying puppies that yap and nip at your ankles.

"I've waited for years for the opportunity to call my time my own," he said. "I've been a good provider. You never had to work outside the home. Are you saying that now, you don't want me to have the chance to enjoy my home like you have for all these years?

"What was she supposed to say? It wasn't as if she minded having him around the house. It was that he simply was driving her crazy with his bossiness and organization compulsion.

"You're driving me crazy, John," she said.

He pushed away from the table and stood up, and left the kitchen without a word.

Then she felt terrible. The man had worked hard for his family at the packing plant, a job he didn't really even like, his entire life. For years, he'd been looking forward to the time he could stay home. She'd hurt his feelings. With the passing of the years, she was getting too set in her ways.

Justine sighed and started to clear the table. She set his dish in the sink, sighed again, and shook her head. She couldn't let him go on feeling like she didn't want him around anymore. She'd put up with him for forty years, she would get through this. Patience and understanding, that's what she needed. She went to find her husband. He deserved an apology.

Cecil Jennings tried not to stare at J.T., but was failing miserably. "So, how long is your cousin going to be in town?" he asked Teddi.

"Indefinitely," J.T. drawled before she could speak. "And by the way we're third cousins, once removed. By marriage," he added.

Cecil looked uncomfortable. Teddi wanted to strangle J.T. Cecil was a member of one of the most prominent African-American families in town, not that there were that many. His brother had been elected mayor for a couple of terms years back, and Cecil was vice president of the local bank. Last year his wife had left him and moved to Wichita. Cecil had shown an interest in Teddi ever since she returned.

Cecil was by far the most attractive African-American man in town, not that she'd ever done anything to encourage him. Apparently something about the situation of Cecil calling on his wife had got J.T.'s masculine competitiveness up. Cecil was intelligent, genuinely nice, and quite attractive, and the poor guy's wife had recently dumped him for goodness sake. She wished J.T. would lighten up.

"Well, I just wanted to wish you a happy new year," Cecil stammered.

Then Eddie swept in, trailing clouds of joy. Teddi was momentarily irritated. Her sister never knocked if the door was open, and in Dixon, there was never much point in locking it.

Cecil's eyes widened. "Edwina," he said, standing and stammering even worse. "It's been years."

"My name is Eddie," she snapped. Then she took a longer look. "Why, Cecil Jennings, you've changed. I heard you married Sally as expected."

"We've just gotten divorced," Cecil said.

"Oh." Teddi saw that Eddie was torn between offering condolences or congratulations. Cecil had dated Sally from grade school through high school, and it was always a given that they would marry. Eddie never could stand Sally.

"Well, I better let myself out," Cecil said. Teddi walked him to the door.

"Take care of yourself this holiday season, I'll see you day after tomorrow here for Kwanzaa?" Teddi asked.

Cecil nodded. "I like the spirit of cultural pride you're bringing to this town. I'll also be at the community Karamu on the thirty-first."

"He sure looks a lot better than he did in high school," Eddie observed as soon as Cecil closed the door behind him.

"I remember he looked good in high school, only Sally had her clutches firmly hooked into him."

"He was so quiet then. Whatever happened to Sally and him?"

"I don't know. Last year she booked for Wichita. I hear she's remarried already."

"Too bad." Then Eddie gave J.T. a mischievous glance. "I see he's interested in your wife."

"I'm not worried," J.T. said, caressing the back of Teddi's neck. "Though I could do without the visits. How often does he come by?"

"Not often. Why did you answer the door? I thought

we were going to keep your presence here quiet," Teddi said.

"Like you said, it's a small town. I don't think there's much point. Everyone knows I'm here already."

Eddie nodded, "That's one thing I hate about this town, everybody's always into your business." She turned to Teddi. "I wanted to see if you wanted to drive to Topeka to do some shopping or something. I'm going stir-crazy."

Teddi looked toward J.T. "No, I'm staying close to home the next few days," she said.

Eddie nodded. "I guess I'll go get Aunt Jenna to go with me, but I thought we'd have more fun."

"I haven't seen my husband in two years, sis," Teddi said.

Eddie nodded. "So, what are you going to do about the bad guys after you?" she asked J.T.

Teddi stifled an urge to roll her eyes. That sentence was obviously the purpose of her whole visit.

"That's our problem," Teddi snapped.

"Touchy, huh? But I guess I don't blame you. You two have a nice evening, happy Kwanzaa."

"You really snapped Eddie's head off," J.T. said after she closed the door.

Teddi sighed. "I know. It's just that I'm worried and on edge. What are we going to do about the bad guys that are after you?"

J.T. folded his arms across his chest and leaned back in the chair. "I think I can access the mainframe once I get into the building, to one of their phone lines. I don't think I really need to get to the computer room. That way, I have a chance."

"But how are you going to get in?" Teddi asked.

J.T. moved next to her. "Don't worry so much, baby, if I can't find a way, I'll make one."

Teddi turned away and started to pace. J.T. poured

himself a glass of ice tea, and settled down on the sofa. "You must be done with your cooking," he said. "You're as nervous as a cat. C'mon over here and talk to me some more," he patted the sofa next to him.

Teddi started to go over to him, but her eye caught the package wrapped in plain brown paper that Wilkins had delivered earlier. She'd completely forgotten about it. She went to pick it up, then she gasped. "J.T., it's addressed to both of us," she said.

Nine

There is no easy walk to freedom anywhere, and many of us will have to pass through the valley of the shadow of death again and again before we reach the mountaintop of our desires.

—*Nelson Mandela*

"Honey, I put labels on all the cabinet shelves. You seem to be having some trouble remembering what's supposed to go where," John said to Justine.

Justine closed her eyes and prayed for the Lord to give her strength.

"Honey?" he asked, concerned. "Are you all right with this? I was relieved when you apologized and said you didn't mind me pitching in to help. I'm really enjoying this. I've been looking forward to getting this place organized for years."

"I'm all right," she said, actually reassuring herself more than him. "The labels will be fine," she added with a weak smile. Patience and understanding, she reminded herself. Patience and understanding.

"I knew you'd be grateful. It's a much better system," John said with enthusiasm. "I'm going to make labels for the shelves in the refrigerator also. You need to make sure you date all the leftovers and discard them after forty-eight hours. I left some markers in the cabinet next to the refrigerator. They're also labeled," he added helpfully.

He took Justine's speechless state for thankful awe. "Don't thank me," he said. "I enjoy helping out. I'm going to go and throw out all the undated leftovers right now."

Justine's hands clenched into fists after he left. May the Lord forgive her, but that man was driving her out of her mind.

Teddi picked up the package and shook it. "It feels heavy, and there's something loose inside."

"Put it down real slow, baby, and come here."

Teddi looked at J.T. wide-eyed, still holding the package. "You don't think it's a bomb?" she said. She set it back on the table and backed away, her eyes on the package.

Then she spun around and ran to get Sylvie.

"Where do you want to go, Mama? I'm going to miss Arthur on TV," Sylvie said.

She and Sylvie met J.T. at the front door. "What are we going to do?" she asked once they were out in the yard.

J.T. looked back at the house. "First we're going to put a few more yards between us and the house," he said.

"We can't call the police," Teddi said.

"You're going to have to." He started to reach for her and she knew it would be a kiss goodbye.

"I have to go," he said. "They may have located me, and it's too dangerous to you to stay."

"No, Daddy, don't go," Sylvie cried, clutching his leg.

"She's right. Wait until we find out more. This is probably just a prank from some kids from the school."

J.T. stared at her. "Have you ever had any pranks like this before?"

She hesitated. "Sure. All the time. I'll call Bud from the neighbor's house, and you can walk Sylvie over to my parents'." Panic washed through her when he didn't move.

"Please," she heard herself pleading.

Her panic was followed by utter relief when she heard J.T. say, "Come on, Sylvie, let's go see Grandma."

"These cans are out of place. The soup is supposed to go *here*, in order; Chicken, mushroom, *then* the tomato," John said patiently to Justine, sounding like he was lecturing a small child.

Justine's entire body stiffened, and her eyes narrowed dangerously. Any man should have quailed at the sight of her, but John's back was turned as he put the soup cans back in order.

"Get out of my kitchen!" she suddenly shrieked.

John jumped straight up in the air and hit his head on the low-hanging cabinet. "What in tarnation is wrong with you, woman?" he asked, his hand cradling his injured temple.

Then he ducked right in time as a glass exploded off the cabinet, near his head. He stared at his wife in disbelief.

"I don't see you moving yet!" She picked up another glass out of the dish drain and let fly.

"You've lost your mind," John said in wonder, and ducked just in time to avoid another missile.

"And you made me lose it! Get out! Get out! Get out!" Justine screamed, punctuating each phrase with a flying glass. She'd run out of glasses, and her eyes moved to the knives in the chopping block.

John got out. "You said you didn't mind if I helped out," he accused, as he quickly left the kitchen. Justine gave a strangled screech and threw a plate after his departing body.

Bud stood in Teddi's yard scratching his head. "They're going to have to send one of them bomb units down from Topeka," he said. "We never had anything like this happen in Dixon before."

Susan Johnson hurried over, steno pad in hand. "Oh, this is so exciting. I've got to interview you for the front page of the *Dixon Journal* tomorrow. Who do you think would send you a bomb addressed to both you and your husband?"

"I have no idea," she said.

"Funny, how that package was mailed from Oklahoma instead of one of them fancy places where you and your ex-husband used to live," Bud said.

Susan gave an arch look at Teddi. "From what I hear, he's still missing isn't he? Your ex-husband must have made plenty of enemies with all that went on two years ago, didn't he?"

"I never divorced him," Teddi whispered.

"What you say there, girl?" Bud asked.

"I never divorced him!" she screamed at the top of her voice.

Bud and Susan looked at each other.

"Why don't you wait at your parents'? I can see that all this is a strain. We'll call you when those boys from Topeka find something," Bud said.

"I'm not going anywhere," she answered. Idiots. Her husband's life was in danger and she was dealing with blithering idiots. She raised her head and let the frigid wind blow in her face. She'd lied to J.T. In all the time he'd been gone, she'd never received anything addressed to him that she didn't expect, like a bill. Why now, when he'd just come back? Who knew about him and who wanted to hurt him? Who wanted to hurt them all if the package was truly a bomb.

A van pulled up filled with men and equipment. They wouldn't let her anywhere near the house until they were done. Mrs. Brown, her neighbor, came over to join the crowd that gathered behind the yellow tape that the police had set up around her front yard.

Teddi was staring at the activity going on around her house mournfully, and didn't hear Mrs. Brown until she shook her shoulder. "A man is on the phone," she said. "He wants to talk to you."

Justine flew up to her bedroom and yanked a suitcase from the closet. Her only thought was to flee from this house before she killed the man. She was too old to do time in prison. She yanked open her drawers and threw clothes in the suitcase.

John stood at the door, looking bewildered. "Why are you so upset? I was just helping out, Justine. You have to admit the house is better organized now."

She saw him through a red haze. "Get . . . out . . . of . . . my sight," she whispered.

He left.

She ran down the stairs, trailing clothes from her suitcase. Her sister, she'd go stay with her sister, she decided. Teddi had problems enough of her own.

The doorbell rang. It'd better not be salespeople or Jehovah's witnesses, she thought, or they'd be sorry. She flung open the door, panting. J.T. and Sylvie stood there.

"What's wrong, Grandma?" Sylvie asked.

Justine grabbed her coat and hat from the hall closet. J.T.'s eyes widened when he saw the suitcase.

"I'm going to stay with my sister for a while," she said.

It was J.T. on the phone. "There seems to be a little problem over at your parents' house," he said. "Your mother's left your dad and gone to stay over at her sister's, and your father is beside himself."

"What?" Teddi said.

"Your mother's—"

"Never mind, I heard you the first time. I simply didn't believe it. They've had blowups before, like in any marriage, but Mama's *never* left Dad."

"Well, she has now. The kitchen is a mess. There's broken glass all over the place."

"Mama did that?"

"Apparently."

"Let me speak to Dad," she said.

"Your mama's done lost her mind over me helping out around the house," John said when he got on the phone.

Teddi closed her eyes. "I'll call her, Dad, and find out what's going on," she said.

He gave the phone back to J.T. "Have the police done anything about the bomb yet?"

"The Topeka Bomb Squad came. They're still in the house. I'll call you as soon as I hear anything."

"All right, baby. I'm going to clean up that kitchen," J.T. said. Teddi said goodbye to J.T. and started to dial Aunt Jenna's house to speak with her mother. What in the world was going on? And why did it have to go on now, with all this happening?

Mrs. Brown stuck her head into the kitchen where

Teddi was on the phone. "There's a man here to see you," she said.

Teddi hung up before she completed the call to her mother, feeling anxious. What did they find?

The man shook her hand. "You're clear to go back home Mrs. Henderson. The package was not a bomb."

"What was it?" she asked. She felt sort of foolish having the bomb squad up here all the way from Topeka when the package was probably a late Christmas present.

"You were right to call us. The person who sent the package definitely had malicious intent, and it could serve as a warning." He pulled a photograph from a clipboard he held and handed it to her.

It was a photograph of a box full of nails and a piece of paper with the words "IT'S A BOMB!" crudely lettered in what looked like crayon.

Teddi drew in her breath. "It's a threat, Mrs. Henderson. We'll be looking into this. The police will want a list of suspects from you, enemies that you or your husband may have."

He turned to leave, then stopped. "You must call if you receive any suspicious or unknown packages. The post office will be keeping an eye out, also," he said. Teddi nodded and shook his hand feeling dazed. A prank—maybe it had only been a prank. Maybe J.T. wouldn't have to leave.

Teddi hugged both Sylvie and J.T. fiercely when they returned home. "Where's Dad?" she asked. She'd told J.T. to bring him over for dinner.

"He wouldn't come," J.T. said. "He was pretty upset, but he tried not to show it. I didn't tell him about the bomb threat, he's got enough on his mind. He was too distracted and worried to even ask why Sylvie and I showed up all of a sudden."

"I just got off the phone with Mama over at Aunt Jenna's. She didn't have much to say except if she lived one more second in that house with that man, she'd have to kill him." Teddi shook her head. "Let me call Dad," she muttered.

What a day. First the mysterious package, and now this. Mama had left Dad for the first time in forty years of marriage. She'd hoped they'd have a happy, peaceful retirement. They'd both worked hard enough through the years to deserve it. But it looked as if Dad's retirement was rocking forty years of love, family, and commitment. Lord, have mercy.

"Why don't you come over for supper tonight?" she asked her father. "It's the second day of Kwanzaa, and I've made some good food."

"Your food's always good. But, no, I need to be here when your Mama comes back. I'm going to give her a piece of my mind for putting me through all this. I'm not getting any younger."

At the rate he was going, if it was up to Mama, he wouldn't be getting any older.

"I'll bring a plate over for you then," Teddi said.

"No, I've got plenty of food. You just enjoy yourself, baby."

Teddi replaced the receiver slowly.

"So, the bomb was a prank?" J.T. said.

Teddi forced a smile on her face. "I told you it would be some kids," she said.

"The police are sure of that?" J.T. asked, watching her.

She nodded. "Of course," she answered.

After they each solemnly took a sip of the water from the kikombe cup, J.T. took the cup and reverently placed it back on the Kwanzaa table. Sylvie stepped forward with the taper Teddi lit and touched it to the candles, first the black, then the red to the left; two candles, one for each day of Kwanzaa.

They sat down to eat after giving thanks. Teddi silently gave additional thanks that they were reunited as a family. The relief Teddi felt didn't quite touch the cold chill of fear she still carried. J.T.'s face was unreadable, but thank God, he was still here with them.

Sylvie glowed with the security of having her father back. She told Teddi earlier in the day that she knew he'd be back, that he wouldn't leave her like that. Then Sylvie added that no matter what she'd done, it couldn't have been bad enough to drive him away forever.

Teddi asked Sylvie to repeat what she said when she heard that. She'd tried so hard to deal with the effects that J.T.'s desertion had on Sylvie, but now she heard that she'd failed miserably. All the time, Sylvie thought something she did wrong drove her daddy away. Teddi had felt like crying.

She felt sick at the thought of how it would affect her daughter if J.T. was snatched away from them again. She didn't have to know how seriously the police were taking the bomb threat. Wasn't it just a prank, after all?

"How is your leg?" J.T. looked up from his plate, which had had his undivided attention for the past few minutes.

"The food is great. Could you pass me some more of the macaroni?"

"Your leg?" Teddi asked again, refusing to allow J.T. to divert her from the subject.

"It's about healed. I told you it was nothing, don't worry about it," J.T. said. "I'd forgotten how good your macaroni and cheese was," he added, changing the subject.

"Cheese and macaroni," Sylvie corrected him.

J.T. smiled at her. "Right," he said.

Teddi realized he was trying hard to keep everything upbeat, and she didn't give voice to her worries. After they ate, they settled down in the living room, classic jazz playing in the background, J.T.'s favorites, Miles Davis and John Coltrane.

"I have a story for the second day of Kwanzaa," she announced. Sylvie grinned and Teddi folded her hands and began her tale.

Living the Nguzo Saba of Self-Determinism: The Story of Sojourner Truth

Sojourner Truth was born named Isabella or Belle in Ulster County, New York, to a Dutch-American owner. When she was still a child, he died and all his livestock— including his slaves, were sold. She never saw her mother again.

Isabella's new masters often physically abused her. Finally, when she was around twelve she was bought by a new and kinder master. He kept for a short while, then sold her for three hundred dollars later to another master who owned a farm. Isabella had grown tall and strong, and she thrived under the hard work.

Forbidding her to marry a slave she loved on a neighboring plantation, her master arranged for her to marry a much older man. She had four children. Her master sold two of her daughters. When he sold off her son, Isabella escaped and found refuge with a Quaker couple.

With the help of the Quakers, she sued the courts for the return of her son from Alabama where he was

taken in violation of state law. Remarkably she wo
her son was returned to her.

She set out for New York City where she worked in menial jobs. One day while scrubbing the floor, she said she heard a message from God. On June 1, 1943, Isabella set out East with only bread, cheese, and twenty-five cents. She renamed herself Sojourner, which means traveler, and Truth for the words she spoke.

She traveled far and wide as an itinerant preacher. Her gift was the truth and the power with which she spoke. She became prominent in the abolitionist movement, and the fire of her oratory lived in many people's hearts and minds and her fame grew great. President Abraham Lincoln received her in the White House. She continued to do good and spread the word until she died, well into her eighties.

Sojourner Truth's life is a shining example of self-determinism. With nothing but her body, soul, and will she created and defined herself, living an extraordinary life, and her voice still echoes, down to this very day.

J.T. and Sylvie sat in silence for a moment, absorbing the story of Sojourner Truth.

Then J.T. cleared his throat. "In the spirit of self-determinism," he said, "I will no longer allow the destiny of this family to be manipulated by outside forces. From this day forward, we as a family will determine our course and stand by our principles, and primarily and foremost, we will never be separated again." J.T.'s voice rang with the force of a vow.

Teddi's heart sang, and right then and there the circle was closed. Her family and heart was whole. J.T. had come back home.

The Third Day of Kwanzaa

The Nguzo Saba is the principle of *UJIMA* (Collective Work and Responsibility)
To build and maintain our community together and to make our sisters' and brothers' problems our problems and to solve them together.

People see God all the time; they just don't recognize him.

—*Pearl Bailey*

Ten

No matter how long the night, the day is sure to come.

—*Congo Proverb*

The night grew cold and blustery, the shimmery blanket of white diamond snow glazed with gray crystal. Inside, J.T. and Teddi stoked inner fires to an uncontrollable blaze that flamed fiercely and now ebbed to the glow of warm embers.

Teddi lay in his arms, replete with loving, intoxicated with the scent of him. Earlier, after the initial happiness over J.T.'s declaration of family unity and self-determination, it seemed as if all Teddi's fears reared their ugly heads at once. What if? What if? What were they going to do? Thoughts had swirled around in her brain like a mad merry-go-round until they peaked to a never-ceasing gnaw at the pit of her stomach. Finally, J.T. gave up trying to reassure her verbally and took her to bed.

That worked better than any pill, Teddi reflected with a smile. Fear was counterproductive. She took a deep breath and decided to leave all her worries with God to carry. After all, they had found the beginnings of a way out. The letter from Paul was truly a miracle, and if J.T. said he could expose the conspiracy, he certainly could do it better than anybody.

But the thought of J.T. going into the government agency where he'd worked for years and left with such infamy still made her sick with fear. She should do it. Unlike J.T., she was anonymous. She'd be unrecognized and nobody would be watching for her. It would be easy for her to get in and access a phone line and the main computer.

She would do it. She'd find a way.

J.T. awoke to the sound of wind whistling and seeking to gain entrance. Teddi's house was well insulated, a haven, shutting evil outside its walls. Unless they invited the evil in. And all those years ago he had.

The sense of betrayal was the worst. Every single other government connection he had turned their backs on him. He was cut off, adrift, *sanctioned*. Except Gerard. His one-time superior gave him an assurance of protection for his family. But even that had been given conditionally, and it had been made clear to him that his family's safety was assured only if he disappeared, virtually died in appearance if not in real life.

Gerard had only given his word after J.T. convinced him that he had no knowledge of what Paul had found. Gerard had power and connections that J.T. couldn't even begin to guess at. But he trusted the man's innate integrity. Gerard always covered his back, and he'd saved Gerard's backside a time or two, also.

He never should have come back. Although then, he never would have found out about Paul's letter, never would have discovered that Paul had left him evidence. Seven days. That's all he wanted and needed. Seven days to renew his spirit before he went out and did what he had to do.

He had to put Paul's spirit to rest, he had to seek justice, not only for himself and his family, but for the harm being done to his people. The harm they allowed to be done to them. J.T. rubbed the bridge of his nose. There was no way he could come to their attention in seven days. Or so he hoped. Before he'd come into Teddi's house he'd watched for signs of surveillance. He had searched the house thoroughly for listening devices. He believed that it was clean, that they'd given up on finding him through his family. After all, he'd disappeared. Maybe they thought that his marriage wasn't that solid, that he had no big stake in his family, and would leave them alone. He had to count on that assumption.

He watched the rise and fall of Teddi's chest with the deep, regular breathing of sleep, her body a dark outline in the night. It was the first night since he'd been back that he'd returned to the familiar sleeplessness that he'd lived with the past two years. Years of anonymous cheap motels, and the constant gnaw of loneliness. Years of frustration as he ran into wall after wall, and wondering if living was worth it. Years when he wanted to curse God for giving him everything and then snatching it away so cruelly.

Two years gone. Two years worth of bitter ashes in his throat. He would gladly kill whoever was responsible and he hated them most of all for that. For giving him his hate back, his fury and his will to kill—a will he thought that Teddi's gentle love had washed away years ago. Oh, yes, he hated, and he could feel their old, scrawny necks cracking in his fists even now.

He soundlessly rolled off the bed and grabbed a pair of sweatpants from the chair, drawing them over his lean hips. Then he made his way to the computer. He had work to do.

Teddi's hands fell into the steady rhythm of chopping onions. Onions seemed to go in almost everything she cooked, the universal flavoring. Onions were like family, ubiquitous, easy to take for granted. You mainly missed them when they were gone.

She was preparing the Jamaican feast she planned to serve that night; more dishes of the diaspora. Food that African people ate in the lands they were scattered to in the New World. For tonight, she had invited people who contributed significant work for the community.

The day was Ujima, collective work and responsibility for one's brothers and sisters. She'd invited them before she had any clue that J.T. would be showing up for Kwanzaa, and now she dearly regretted it.

Tomorrow, they were going to drive up to Topeka. Teddi had planned a shopping spree from the African-American merchants there, but she hadn't counted on how difficult it would be to find more than one or two. They'd do a little shopping at the one mall there tomorrow, a nice mall with several high-end department stores. She and J.T. needed to get out of the house, inhale some fresh air, and stretch, but now Teddi was reluctant to go, to allow the world to intrude on the haven they'd created.

The phone rang, and Teddi rinsed the scent of onions from her hands before answering. "I'm going stir-crazy," Eddie said.

"How is it over at the folks'?"

"Dad's moping around. He refuses to go see Mama, and when I called her, she refused to talk to him." Eddie's voice lowered to a whisper. "She broke near every glass in the kitchen. I couldn't believe it. Maybe I do take after her, after all."

"J.T. told me. He cleaned up the mess."

"According to Dad she went completely off for no good reason, other than him helping her out. And he acts like he doesn't have a clue why."

"That's unlikely. Mom wouldn't go off without a better reason than that."

"She told me he drove her crazy," Eddie said.

"That's what she told me, but it wouldn't take forty years for Mama to realize that Dad drives her crazy. There must be another reason."

"I don't think so. She said she was thinking of a separation. She doesn't think she can live with him anymore."

"What?" Teddi said. "You're not telling me Mama's thinking of leaving him? After forty years?"

"I don't see how they can stand it around here. All they do is eat and sit around doing crossword puzzles," Eddie said. "I'm surprised they don't weigh three hundred pounds each. I've gained four pounds. I'm frantic!"

"We're not talking about you. I doubt that them eating too much has anything to do with Mama threatening to leave Dad," Teddi said.

"I'm coming over, maybe we can go over to see Mama," Eddie paused. "You have any of that Jamaican food done?" she asked.

"I've lived with your father too long to want to hurt him," Justine said.

"But you are hurting him, Mama," Eddie said.

Justine looked at her sideways. "I meant physically."

"You couldn't hurt Dad physically," Eddie said.

"You think not?" she answered.

"What I want to know is what Dad did that made you so angry?" Teddi asked.

Justine looked at her hands. "He made me a schedule," she mumbled.

"What?" Teddi asked.

"He made me a schedule," Justine said louder. "He rearranged everything in my house. He even rearranged my kitchen!"

"Ohhh," Eddie said.

Teddi shook her head. Dad had really messed up this time, she thought.

Teddi walked with Eddie over to their parents' house after they left Aunt Jenna's.

"After Dad apologizes to Mama, I'll spring for a weekend at a four-star hotel in Kansas City for them, with champagne, flowers, the works," Eddie said.

"Mama and Dad aren't about to go to any hotel, you know that," Teddi said. "Though the champagne and flowers wouldn't be a bad idea," she added.

"Dad has to go to Mama on his knees and humbly beg her forgiveness, that's the main thing."

"And what makes you think Dad is going to do that? He doesn't think he did anything wrong," Teddi said. Then she laughed. "Remember when Dad reorganized our Barbie doll things?"

"We didn't talk to him for a week," Eddie said, chuckling.

"It was okay when Dad kept his organizational tendencies on the job, but I shudder to think how it is now that he's home all the time," Teddi said.

"We'll talk to him. He's a reasonable man," Eddie said. Teddi looked at her. "Usually," she added.

"Should we talk to him together?" Teddi asked.

"No, let me approach him alone first. I'll send for reinforcements if needed."

"All right. What are you doing this evening?" Teddi asked.

"I've read two books already, and I'm starting on a third."

"We've spent a lot of time meditating and reading also. Kwanzaa is a time for reflection."

"I've reflected so much, I'm about ready to melt down," Eddie complained. "I wish you'd drive up to Kansas City with me, but I don't blame you not wanting to forsake your little love nest. If I hadn't gotten any for two years, I wouldn't want to come out of the house either."

Teddi sucked on her teeth in irritation. "That's not all of it."

"You're still worried about that cloak-and-dagger stuff?"

"Yeah, I'm worried, wouldn't you be?"

Eddie was quiet for a moment. "I guess I would be, but what are you going to do? I'll be honest. I'm totally fascinated by all that's going on in your life, and while I dearly love spending time with the folks, I'm hanging around to see how it all turns out."

Then changing the subject, Eddie asked, "What are you doing for Kwanzaa tonight?"

"I'm inviting a few people who work in and for the community. Want to come?"

"Sounds interesting," Eddie's tone saying exactly the opposite. "Cecil called and asked me out," she said, a little too casually.

"Are you going?"

"I suppose I will to pass the time. We're going to drive to Kansas City."

"He's a nice guy," Teddi said meaningfully. Don't hurt him, was the message beneath the words.

"I'm bored around here. I need a little fun." I don't care; back off, was Eddie's unspoken answer. "Though nice was never my cup of tea," Eddie added.

That's your problem, sis. That's exactly why you're alone at thirty-two through two marriages and countless relationships. Teddi would never say the words aloud. They cut too close to the bone not to wound her sister.

"Have a good time," Teddi said.

"I plan to."

Eleven

We have the right and, above all, we have the duty
to bring strength and support of our entire community to defend the lives and property of each individual family.

—*Paul Robeson*

"Hey, Dad, you home?" Eddie called.

"In here," John called from the kitchen.

When Mama was there she filled the whole kitchen.
Dad looked small sitting at the kitchen table drinking
a cup of coffee.

Eddie poured herself a cup of coffee and sat across
from him. "Did you eat dinner?"

"I'm not hungry," he said.

"You've got to eat something." John didn't reply and
the words sat there, meaning nothing.

"I just got back from talking to Mama," she said. "She
told me what the problem is."

John took a sip of his coffee. Eddie saw that he was
trying to act like it didn't matter. She let a few seconds
pass.

"And?" he said.

Eddie smiled inwardly. She knew Mama was the only thing that really mattered to him at this moment.

"You know how you like to put things in order?" Eddie asked.

He nodded, impatient.

"Well, it drives Mama crazy."

"Is that it?" he demanded. "She said she didn't mind."

"She did mind, but she didn't want to hurt your feelings."

"The woman goes completely berserk, leaves me for the first time in forty years because I do some organization around here?"

"You've never been home all the time in forty years either," Eddie replied.

"That's what it is. She doesn't want me around," he said, real pain starting to show on his face.

"That's not it, Dad. It's the reorganizing thing. It would drive anyone nuts. You rearranged her kitchen for God's sake. You never, but never rearrange a woman's kitchen."

"I was only trying to help."

"It didn't help, Dad."

He sighed. "So what am I supposed to do now?" he said, mainly to himself.

Eddie took his hand. "Find something to occupy your time with something other than the house. It's been Mama's castle for forty years and it's dangerous to try to change that." Eddie brightened as an idea came to her. "Have you ever thought about running a business? Folks in L.A. spend a fortune to have someone come in and get their garages and attics in order."

"That's something to think about. But for right now, I'm worried about how I'm going to get your Mama to come back home."

"If romance doesn't work, begging might. I'd try

both. And I suggest you put the kitchen back the way it was."

"Everybody knows someone is here anyway. It's going to be more suspicious if we try to hide you," Teddi said to J.T. "This is a small town, some people will make it their mission to find out what really is going on if we don't seem open." Like that mailman Wilkins, she thought.

J.T. nodded. "I never saw much point in trying to hide. If they were still looking for me, I'd know it by now." A wry smile crossed his face. "Also, you have a big family, baby. It's inevitable that the news about me will travel soon."

Teddi nodded, thinking about the package she'd received. The package was nothing, a box of nails, a silly note. Surely nobody serious, the mysterious "they," would fool around with that type of thing. It was likely just a prank after all, and nothing to worry about. Teddi shivered.

The ring of the doorbell interrupted her dark thoughts. "Lord, I'm not ready yet," she said. "Would you answer the door?" she asked J.T.

She headed for the bedroom and heard the three teachers that she'd invited for the Kwanzaa celebration greet her husband. J.T. with his fine self would make a good piece of gossip. Eligible men were rare in this town, and most of the single women who dated saw men from Topeka or Kansas City. They'd be abuzz wondering where she found him. Teddi sighed and hurriedly put the finishing touches on her makeup.

When she emerged from the bedroom, almost all the guests had arrived. She'd invited people whose work made a difference in the community. A woman who ran a food pantry for the needy cradled her drink, chatting to another woman who gave tremendous assistance to battered women through the town's resource center for women. The minister of her parents' church was present, also a man who was one of the social workers at the community mental health center.

The invitations had been issued before J.T. came on the scene, and with a sense of dismay Teddi spied Bud, the policeman, deep in conversation with Wilkins, the mailman.

"Habari gani means 'what's the news?' " Teddi announced to the group.

Conversation ceased, and everyone in the room turned to her. "Today the response is Ujima," she continued. "Ujima is the Nguzo Saba, or the principle, we're remembering today, the principle of collective work and responsibility. I've specifically invited you all here to share the Kwanzaa meal with me because all of you take responsibility for helping others in the community in some way.

"I've served a buffet of foods from Jamaica, a land where many African people settled after being torn from their native country, and where the native cuisine, along with the culture, has been influenced by Africa. Afterward there will be a short ceremony, and I know better than to try to observe any rituals on empty stomachs, so let's eat!"

A unanimous murmur of approval rose, and the group moved toward the delicious aroma of food set out on the buffet table to help themselves.

"Daddy, will you serve my plate?" asked Sylvie, her voice echoing through the dining room. Conversation paused for a moment, the resumed after a slight hesitation. Teddi closed her eyes for a moment, feeling agitated. What should she say to these people? Fortunately only a very few knew of the circumstances of J.T.'s defection, one of them was their minister, the other was the social worker. She didn't miss the startled glances both of them sent in J.T.'s direction.

Compliments and requests for recipes abounded for Teddi's meal. When everyone was about done, J.T. lifted the kikombe cup, gave honor to the ancestors, and poured the libation. He passed the cup, and everyone sipped from it in a moment of solemn reflection. Sylvie lit the candles in the kinara.

"I've asked Reverend Perry to tell us a story," Teddi announced.

The reverend approached the Kwanzaa table and cleared his throat. He lowered himself to a comfortable chair Teddi had set next to the Kwanzaa table for the storyteller. The atmosphere of the room had eased to a warm and mellow glow with good food, soft African voices singing in the background, candlelight, and the fragrance of incense.

"Teddi asked me to speak about collective work and responsibility, but tonight I feel called to speak to you about the story of David and Goliath," Reverend Perry said.

"Amen," a few voices from the audience called.

The reverend launched into the story of the shepherd boy who loved playing the harp. As he told the story of how the youth's bravery and faith in God led him to defeat a giant fearsome warrior in single combat, he grew quite worked up. The "Amen's" and "Yes, Lord's" grew louder, and Teddi's living room took on the aura of Sunday morning at church.

The reverend ended the story with a flourish, saying how David's faith led him to become King and lead Israel to prosperity and happiness the war-torn country had never known before, and Teddi felt her heart lift a little.

The odds her family faced made Goliath the giant dwindle into Goliath the dwarf. If David's faith could lead a whole nation home, maybe faith could lead J.T. out of this mess.

Then, Wilkins sidled up to her and whispered in her ear. "I've been wanting to tell you something," he said. "I'm sure you're not aware that you're harboring a wanted man here. But don't worry, I told Bud, and he's going to take care of everything, discreet-like."

Teddi saw Bud moving by the front door, probably so J.T. couldn't bolt.

"He's my husband and he was framed," she whispered to Wilkins, tears coming to her eyes. Her worst fears were coming true.

"Everybody come and listen to Sylvie's story," J.T.'s voice cut through the room.

Sylvie sat proudly in the chair by the Kwanzaa table. "I'm going to tell the story of Harriet Tubman, who lived the principle of working to help and being responsible for other people."

Teddi could hardly see her daughter through the film of tears that clouded her eyes. She wanted to tell J.T. to run, to get away. She didn't think Bud would shoot him, but then again she couldn't be sure. A heavy paralysis came over her.

"Harriet Tubman was born a slave around 1820," Sylvie said.

"Her grandparents had been brought from Africa. Her master was very mean to her and made her work hard and beat her often. When she was fifteen she saw another slave run away. She got in the way of the man chasing him, and the man hit her in the head with a piece of iron so hard, she almost died.

"In 1849 she heard news that she and her brothers were going to be sold South, even though she was married to a free man. So she ran away at night following the North star. Her two brothers soon turned back, but

Harriet kept on. Kind people of all races helped her on her journey. She finally reached Pennsylvania.

"She worked hard in Pennsylvania. She wanted badly to get her parents out of the South and slavery. She became a conductor on the Underground Railroad. The Underground Railroad was a network of people and places to help slaves escape North. She went South and helped slaves run away North so many times she was called Moses, and the reward on her head was forty-thousand dollars. But she kept on working to help people. She helped many of her own family get free from slavery.

"In 1850 her work became harder because the government passed a law saying that runaway slaves up North had to be returned to their owners. There were many jobs as slave-catchers because the slave owners would pay for each returned slave, and it became very dangerous for the ex-slaves. Now slaves had to run all the way to Canada for freedom.

"Harriet Tubman worked hard for the Union army in the Civil war. After the war she returned to a small house she'd bought in Auburn, New York. She met many important people who worked against slavery and she worked against slavery and for African-American people until she died when she was ninety-three years old. The end."

The room broke into applause. Sylvie jumped out of the chair and buried her face in her father's shirt.

Bud approached J.T. Teddi's heart beat in slow motion. Thud. "Come with me. We have some things to talk about," Bud said.

Thud. A collective gasp went up from the guests.

"No, no, no, you're not going to take my daddy away again," Sylvie screamed.

Teddi couldn't breath or move. Bud hesitated, looking abashed.

J.T. had frozen also, eyes narrowed, looking down at Bud. Teddi knew he was poised for action. Teddi also knew what quick, violent action he could make. But Bud had the gun.

"She's right. J.T.'s not going anywhere, Bud." Fear caused Teddi to find her voice. "I invited you as a guest in my home. J.T. is my husband and Sylvie's father, and we're a family. We will not be separated again, and this is why."

Teddi sat down in the storyteller's chair like a queen. A hush fell over the room. Bud backed away from J.T., and it was with palpable relief that Teddi saw the tension drain from J.T. Wilkins still stood, looking between Bud and J.T. "But the law . . ." he started to say.

"Sit down, Wilkins, and at least hear Teddi out," Bud said.

Teddi saw the still-resolute set of J.T.'s features. There was no way he was going to allow Bud to take him in. At the very least, he'd be on the run again. It was up to her. Teddi took a deep breath and began to speak.

Twelve

If you burn a house, can you conceal the smoke?
　　　　　　　　　　　　　—Bugunda proverb

She relayed to them everything J.T. had confessed to her family. The guests were rapt.

Bessie Wilson, one of the teachers, sighed into the silence after Teddi was done. "How romantic and exciting. Nothing like that would ever happen to me."

Bud put his hands on his thighs and rocked back and forth. "Well, maybe we should give you the benefit of the doubt," he said slowly. Then he shot a look at Wilkins. "I had a long talk with John Thompson the other day. He told me that all isn't always what it seems on the surface. He told me a few things about his son-in-law then. Besides, Teddi said this matter will be cleared up one way or another in a few days. The Thompsons are good people, and they vouch for him. I never much cottoned to the government anyway."

"Amen," said Reverend Perry softly. "Remember the story of David and Goliath, though I never imagined it would be so appropriate."

Teddi slowly exhaled. She had done it, she thought.

She turned the tide. Maybe the town would rally around her family. At least not report J.T. to federal authorities. She saw no reason why anyone would take the trouble.

At that moment the earth shook, and screams erupted as everyone ran to the sliding glass doors to see what was happening. Teddi noticed that J.T. grabbed Sylvie and ran in the opposite direction, toward the front of the house. Turning to follow her husband, her attention was caught by the gasps of the people staring out the back. Orange flames reflected on their faces from the inferno that blazed where her garage used to be.

"Oh, no!" Andrea, one of the teachers exclaimed. "Teddi was storing our boat in that garage."

"Stay back everybody," Bud muttered and drew his gun.

"Did someone call 911?" Mike, the social worker, asked.

"I'm here already," said Bud, sounding a little miffed.

"So am I," chimed in Wilkins, a member of the volunteer fire brigade.

"I'm going to call 911," Mike said.

Teddi ran to the front of her house to where J.T. and Sylvie had disappeared. They were no longer in the house.

John held his hat in his hands as he stood in front of Jenna's door. "May I speak to Justine?" he asked.

Jenna stood aside to let him in.

"Justine, your husband is here to see you," she called.

John waited in the tiny living room. An old black and white movie was on the television. He felt more nervous than he'd been in a long time. You never realize what you have, until you've almost lost it.

Justine entered and it caught in his throat how beautiful she was. Funny he never noticed her beauty until she left, never felt how empty the house was without her in it until she was gone.

"What do you want?" she asked, her tone neutral.

He sat on the couch. He cleared his throat, wanting to say the right thing to this woman he'd shared the past forty years with. He wanted to say the things that would make her come back to him. "Won't you sit down?" he asked. "I'd like to talk to you."

Justine sat in the chair farthest from him.

"First, I want to say I'm sorry. I'm sorry I made a schedule for you and reorganized your kitchen. You've kept the house just fine for forty years. I was just filling my time," he said. "I want you to come home," he finished, the words coming out in a rush.

The silence grew and filled the room, almost choking him. He longed to drop words into it, but he waited for her to break the still.

"I accept your apology, but sorry don't mean anything is going to change. I can't live with you driving me crazy the rest of my life," she finally said.

John looked down. "I called Mitch Green," he said. "He said that he would be more than happy to have me help organize his inventory. I figure a lot of people need help to get their things in order. Eddie mentioned something about me starting a business. I suppose that would take up a lot of my time, get me out of the house."

"I suppose it would," she said, leaning back in her chair staring at John, a smile slowly forming on her face. "So you really do understand," she said.

"I put your kitchen back the way it was before."

"Unalphabetized cans and all?"

John nodded. A rich, deep chocolate laugh, identical to her daughter Teddi's rumbled out from within her, and she stood up.

"I'll get my things together," she said.

John moved close to her and caressed her cheek. They stood like that for a while and there was no need for any more words. The years passed, and they grew older, but the love between them never aged, and couldn't pass away.

"Tell me again exactly where you were when you heard the explosion," the Dixon fire chief asked Teddi for the third time.

"I've told you and everybody else in this town everything there is to tell. I want you to find my husband and my child," Teddi's voice rose.

"There, there," the fireman said. "Bud is out right now searching for them. Don't you worry, Mrs. Henderson," he continued. "Seeing your place get bombed and all, that puts a different light on things. Now, I bet nobody says a thing about your husband. The people in this town aren't about to allow sinister gov'ment forces to hound one of our own. We never have before, and we aren't going to start now."

Overwhelmed, Teddi started to cry. Where was her daughter, J.T.? The phone rang.

"It's your mother," Andrea called from the kitchen.

"Mama . . ." Teddi started to say, her voice breaking.

"I want to tell you that J.T. brought Sylvie over to the house where she'd be safe," her mother cut in.

"Thank God," Teddi breathed. "Is J.T. over at Aunt Jenna's too?"

"No, he left right after he dropped Sylvie off. He told me no one was hurt. I'm not at Aunt Jenna's anymore, I'm at the house. J.T. told me to call you right away to let you know Sylvie's all right. She was pretty upset about the explosion."

"You're with Dad?" Teddi asked, confused.

"I'm at the house, aren't I?" her mother answered.

"Did he tell you where he was going?" Teddi asked.

"No. I thought he'd be back at your place by now. It took a minute or two to settle Sylvie down."

"When did you go back to Dad, Mama?"

"I just got here. You know, it seems to me that you have enough problems of your own to deal with," Justine said.

Your parents' marriage is not your business, is what her mother was saying. She set the receiver down slowly. Her mama was right, she did have enough problems of her own to worry about. Dread settled in the pit of her stomach. Was this the end? Did J.T. leave her without saying goodbye?

Cecil held the door of the jazz club open for Eddie. She was glad she'd decided to wear the black dress instead of the red one. You couldn't go wrong with a little black dress, real diamonds, and her ever-present Joy perfume. The scent was classic, expensive, and elegant like she was tonight. She'd toned herself down especially for Cecil. She didn't know if he could handle Eddie in full force. Most men couldn't. Now that didn't mean they didn't try.

So far, Cecil had been a perfect gentleman. Dinner had been delightful. Verbal but soft spoken, intelligent but somewhat shy, he was an interesting man. He had seemed fascinated with her. He'd asked her questions about her life, and her thoughts and feelings, and really listened to her responses. Eddie knew how rare it was to find a man who didn't want to impress you with tales about himself, especially on the first date. She tried to ask Cecil about himself, tried to sneak up on the subject of his marriage and Sally, but he was reticent, skillfully redirecting the conversation back to her.

He'd tried not to stare as she used her tongue to extract the last bit of succulent lobster from its shell. He wanted her, but then again, most men did. She wondered what moves he would make on her, and felt a tingle deep within at the thought. Cecil Jennings was an intriguing man. Much more intriguing than she thought she'd find out here in the wilds of Dixon, Kansas.

The jazz club was dark, intimate, and smoky. Eddie usually hated cigarette smoke at any time, for any reason, but the haze seemed to be right here in this club. Couples were dancing, a singer, an attractive woman with a head wrap à la Erykah Badu crooned a blues ballad.

"Dance with me," Eddie said, holding out her hand to Cecil. He hesitated and then led her out on the dance floor. He drew her into his arms, and Eddie relaxed against his shoulder. Their bodies fit together nicely. She inhaled his scent, soap overlaid with a woodsy aftershave.

This was feeling just a tad too good, she thought. She dated actors, screenwriters, and other Hollywood players who were up on their luck. That was the sort of man she was attracted to, fun and exciting, on the cutting edge of style, plenty of money and flash. Not this man from a tiny town in Kansas who dated the same girl all through school and worked at a bank.

Cecil stopped moving and Eddie realized the song had ended. The band started to play a more upbeat, jazzy number. He still held her, dancing the old-fashioned way. "Why didn't you date anybody else but Sally during high school?" Eddie asked.

"Habit. Her family lived next door to mine. We'd played together as long as I could remember. I knew a lot of things about her," he said.

"So, you knew all her secrets?" Eddie said lightly.

Cecil didn't smile as he nodded. "I knew all her secrets," he replied.

They didn't talk much on the drive back to Dixon, but the silence was companionable and easy. Eddie understood better why Sally'd kept her hooks firmly engaged in this man all through high school. There was something about him that appealed to every feminine sense she had, the better she got to know him.

When they rolled into Dixon, Eddie could tell that he was heading to her parents' house to drop her off. "I'd rather stop by your place for a drink, than go home to my empty bed," Eddie purred.

Cecil looked over at her, but he didn't turn the car around. "I had a good time tonight, and I'd like to see you again," he said. "But I need to take it slow. Sally recently left and . . ."

"What does me and you have to do with Sally?" Eddie asked.

Cecil shifted in his seat. "Nothing, really. I guess I'm not ready to take any relationship to that level yet."

Not ready? What was wrong with him? 'He was starting to piss her off. Cecil pulled up to her parents' house.

"Goodbye, Eddie," he said. "I had a wonderful time."

She stared at him in disbelief. The man was dropping her off at home when she said she was willing to go to his place.

"I'll call you," he said when Eddie showed no sign of moving.

Then Eddie grabbed her purse and got out of the car. "Don't bother," she snarled, slamming the car door as hard as she could behind her. She was gratified to see him wince.

The Fourth Day of Kwanzaa

The Nguzo Saba is the principle of *UJAMMA*
(Cooperative Economics)
To build and maintain our stores, shops, and other businesses and to profit from them together.

Economics do not dictate a level of intelligence.
However, economics do dictate opportunity.

—*Bill Cosby*

Thirteen

The dawn of a new day is upon us and we see things differently. We see now not as individuals, but as a collective whole, having one common interest.

—*Marcus Garvey*

Teddi believed J.T. could walk away from them again, but she never believed that he would leave without saying goodbye. She blindly stumbled away from the people who filled her house and lay on her bed in the dark. She welcomed the numbness that filled her, it was better than the pain that would soon rack her.

Then, someone sat next to her on the bed. She must have slept.

"Baby."

Teddi's eyes flew open and she sat upright, wrapping her arms around his neck. "Oh, God, J.T. I knew you wouldn't leave me like that. I couldn't bear it."

He kissed her. "I have to go, Teddi. That was a warning," he said.

"Why would anybody bother to warn you? You said they were afraid of what you could reveal, wouldn't they just get rid of you if they knew where you were?"

"That's what bothers me," he said.

"It doesn't make any sense. Please don't run away until we find out what's going on," she pleaded.

"I'm not running away," J.T. said. "I'm trying to protect my family."

"We can do this together," she said.

He hesitated, then nodded slowly. "I'm not underestimating you, baby. I know you're a strong woman. It's that this is all my fault . . ."

"Is it?" Teddi asked. "Is it really? I wanted the American Dream. I wanted my family to see that I had 'made it.' I wanted the big house in the suburbs and the Jeep Cherokee and the fancy vacations, all the things money could buy. If I hadn't wanted all those things, would you still have felt compelled to work for the government? When we got married, you told me you wanted to get out."

"I wanted those things for us, too, baby. It's not your fault."

"It's not your fault either, don't you see? It's our fault. We need to stick together and get through this thing as a family. Please don't split us apart again, I'm begging you."

She molded her body to his and he wrapped his arms around her, his breath moist on her face. "I'm begging you," Teddi whispered.

J.T. made a sound of surrender deep in his throat and his mouth lowered to touch hers. Then, a volley of knocks sounded on the door.

"Are you folks finished in there?" Bud called. "The captain wants to talk to you."

"I think we should set up a watch around the house," Mike, the social worker, said after the police captain had interviewed J.T. and they were all gathered in the living room again.

"You understand we'll have to keep this quiet and all, him being a wanted man. Like I said, the captain won't mind sitting on this a few days, but J.T. is going to have to move quick to take care of things. We'll make sure the little one is safe," Bud said.

Gratitude replaced the astonished disbelief on J.T.'s face, and he exhaled slowly. "I will set this all straight right after Kwanzaa. You people have no idea what this means to me, your placing your trust in a stranger."

"You're no stranger. You're Teddi's husband, Sylvie's father, and God help you, Justine's son-in-law," Reverend Perry said. "Don't go running back to New York City when this is all over. You and Teddi belong right here in Dixon."

Her heart spilled over with gratitude. She was one of Dixon's own, and the people descended from hard-working, no-nonsense farmers rallied around someone they considered one of their own, no matter what color, especially if it was the government who opposed them. The people of Dixon had always been a fiercely independent lot, slow to follow along with the mood and means of the rest of the nation. Dixon was where they belonged and her family wasn't going anywhere.

The next morning, the police wanted them out of the house to go over the area for evidence once more. They'd all spent the night at Teddi's parents', then decided to go shopping at the Topeka mall like they'd previously planned. Life went on, and the attack wasn't serious. J.T. had said again he didn't know why anyone would bother to give him a warning.

"Daddy! Can I go there?" Sylvie cried, pointing to a store packed with whirling and buzzing wind-up and battery-operated toys.

They all crossed to the store, and Sylvie took off in delight to see all the different movements of the toys.

Teddi and J.T. wandered around the store, and while J.T. purchased a parrot that flapped its wings and swung from its perch, Teddi stood in front of a cymbal-clapping monkey and stared aimlessly out of the plate glass window.

Her attention was drawn to two uniformed policemen, walking slowly perusing the shoppers, obviously looking for someone. Her heart beat faster. She realized how unlikely it would be for the police in Topeka to be looking for J.T. If someone tipped them off, they could have easily picked him up at the house. Nevertheless she felt relieved when J.T. made the purchase. When he walked out, J.T. glanced around seemingly nonchalantly, but Teddi knew he was always aware of every nuance of his surroundings, including the policemen. She was relieved when they walked in the opposite direction from the policemen.

They ate lunch in the food court. Teddi was a little disheartened that she hadn't found one African-American-owned shop to purchase anything from on this day of Ujamma, cooperative economics. She'd heard that there was an African-American-owned barbecue around, but it was only open for supper, an African-American-owned night club was that basically a hole in the wall, and another business that they were leaving for after they ate, an art and clothing shop.

Teddi had a friend who went to a Chamber of Commerce breakfast in Topeka and didn't see a single face of color there. It was a shame. Like many places in the United States, African-Americans had representation in state and local government and in the nonprofit sector, but very little in the economic arena, where the power lay.

"I bet it's a whole lot easier to buy drugs and guns

in Topeka, than to buy from legitimate African-American businesses," J.T. said.

"It is. It's near impossible for an African-American to get a business loan from a local bank here. Hardly any of us are hooked into their network," Teddi murmured. "Though there's not many of us, percentage-wise," she added.

J.T.'s features were grim, and she knew he was thinking about the guns channeled into African-American neighborhoods to fund illicit activities in the government. Teddi wondered how one man could put a stop to what was a pervasive nationwide problem. It looked hopeless. J.T. would be lucky to get out of this mess alive, much less being able to topple the influential kingpins who had a substantial part in running the country. And nobody was forced to buy a gun or drugs, anyway.

She didn't want to think about it. At least not until after Kwanzaa. But the shadow of fear loomed like a dreaded beast just barely out of sight, merely awaiting the opportunity to pounce and devour. She shivered. Suddenly, Teddi couldn't wait to get back to the sanctuary of her home.

"Honey, you should have seen the money that man spent on me last night," Eddie said, draping herself over the breakfast bar at their parents' house.

Teddi stirred the batter of the injera bread she was preparing for that evening and murmured noncommittally. She loved cooking in her mother's kitchen. The memories were good and strong, seasoning the food, easing her soul.

Dad and Mama took Sylvie and went out shopping for some more glasses, among other things. Her parents had been cooing like lovebirds all day. Nothing like a good fight to remember how good making up can be, she thought. And she'd never seen her parents have such a fight.

"He only took me to the best," Eddie continued. "I had the lobster and the best cut of steak. If I knew I could have had such a good time in Kansas City, I might have never left for L.A. Shoot, by the time we got home that man deserved some of me."

Now, Eddie had Teddi's full attention. "You slept with him?" Teddi asked, a tone of dismay in her voice.

"No, it still would have been a mercy f—"

"Eddie! Cecil is a nice a man. I was concerned because he doesn't deserve to be jerked around by you."

"Cecil is a big boy, he doesn't need Mama Teddi looking out after him. And he'd be delighted with any jerking I cared to do to him. I plan to see a lot of him. Quite a lot," Eddie said with a coy smile.

Teddi shook her head in defeat. Eddie always did exactly as she wanted, especially when it came to men. Something about what she told her about Cecil didn't ring quite true. She probably teased him and played hard to get last night, leaving him hot and bothered and tied up in knots. The sad thing was poor Cecil's heart would be in more of a shambles than it already was from Sally when Eddie finished with him. She'd be way too much for him.

"Whatever it is you're cooking smells mighty good, but it doesn't look like anything I recognize. What are you making there? Pancakes?" Eddie said referring to the batter Teddi was pouring into the hot griddle.

"No, Ethiopian bread. I'm cooking food from Ethiopia and Egypt, lands where our people once had great civilizations."

Eddie wrinkled her nose. "I was hoping you were doing Caribbean food again. I'll be here tonight with Cecil. The town is buzzing about J.T. He's becoming quite famous. Abner Wilson was laying up ammo, to 'fight the sinister gov'ment forces coming to our town,' in his own quaint words."

"I'm worried sick that he will get too famous. The danger is real, Eddie. And neither of us has been exactly discreet."

Eddie shrugged. "It would take longer than the few days J.T. going to be here for the news to travel from Dixon," Eddie said.

"Not necessarily. You heard of phones, faxes, computer modems? And what about my garage being blown up by a bomb!"

"Well, it would have been the house if anyone really wanted to hurt you. Mike Deaver is organizing a watch. They'd spot any federal types right off. Boy, this is the most exciting thing to happen in this town for years. Susan wanted to make it a front page story in the Dixon paper, but Bud persuaded her to wait until J.T. is gone."

All Teddi could do was sigh, and go on preparing her dinner.

Fourteen

An Italian comes over here from his country to repair
shoes in a community of Negroes, and the Greeks to
feed them, the Chinese to wash their clothes, and
the Jew to sell their merchandise. . . . If we permit
foreigners to impoverish us by establishing and con-
trolling businesses (in the black community) which
we support, then we ought to starve.

—*Carter G. Woodson, Ph.D.*

J.T. went through the house a second time, his agita-
tion evident in every move he made. Then again, maybe
not. Once he'd believed the trail was cold. But now,
every sense in his body screamed danger. His fear was
that something alien had invaded Teddi's home. His
home.

He stopped by the Kwanzaa table, running his hands
carefully under the edges. Nothing. The worst scenario
was that they suspected his presence. They couldn't
know where he was yet. If they knew, they would have
come to get him already.

He had no business here, endangering those he loved
most. He'd have to go. He'd tell Teddi as soon as she

returned from the store. A long, sweet goodbye. A lump settled in his chest.

J.T. flinched as the doorbell sounded. He slid a gun into the back waistband of his pants and peered out the window. The postman's moon-shaped red face was outside the door. He impatiently rang the doorbell again.

J.T. opened the door. "Can I help you?" he asked.

Wilkins looked about nervously. "I wanted to talk to you. But not here, could we take a walk?"

An alarm sounded within J.T., and his lips thinned. Why would the mailman want to walk outside in frigid twenty degree weather any more than his job required? He needed to find out. J.T. got his coat. He had no fear of this overplump, perspiring U.S. mailman.

The look of relief on the mailman's face was almost comical when J.T. followed him out.

"Let's walk down this way," the mailman gestured down a quiet residential street. J.T. nodded and they set out, only observed by the gray Kansas skies.

Teddi let herself into her home. One night away and the air inside of the house felt stale and old. No more a sanctuary, the life had faded from her home. Teddi shook her head. One meal cooked in the kitchen would make this house her home again. J.T. insisted that they stay away from the house, so she was going to cook and have the Kwanzaa celebration at her parents'. She'd stopped to get the kinara, candles, and other items she'd collected for Kwanzaa. She got the wooden box and started to pack the things. A creak made her pause for a moment. She shook her head, and continued. Nerves . . . she was jumpy. It was the house settling, that's all. Finishing her task, she picked up the box and straightened.

The box crashed to the floor as Teddi saw the large decorative mirror that faced the Kwanzaa table. "Get out of town and stay out, you sorry slut," was written in ugly red lipstick across the mirror.

Wilkins struggled to keep up with J.T.'s long strides. He kept darting nervous glances at him, but J.T. wasn't about to initiate the conversation. The man said he wanted to talk to him.

"I wanted to tell you . . . to tell you—listen could you slow down a little?" Wilkins asked, panting.

J.T. slowed down.

"I saw someone at your house last night. I know that you and your wife were at her parents', and a light came on in the living room for a few minutes." He looked up at J.T. "I also saw a figure in black skulking around your backyard," he added when J.T didn't say anything.

"Did you call the police?" J.T. asked.

"Nooo. If it was government agents I didn't see the point. I just wanted to warn you that your house is probably bugged. That's why I didn't want to talk to you in the house."

J.T. nodded. "Thank you very much for your concern, Mr. Wilkins," he said.

"Hi, Mommy," Sylvie said as she let Teddi into her parents' house.

"You need some help?" Eddie asked approaching the door.

"Grandpa and I are going to watch a movie he rented," Sylvie announced, skipping away. Eddie helped Teddi carry in the groceries she'd bought earlier and the Kwanzaa box. "I think Dad loves it when Sylvie visits because it gives him an excuse to watch all those Disney cartoons," she said. Then she looked closely at her sister. "What's wrong with you?" she asked. "You look like you've seen a ghost."

"Somebody's been in my house," Teddi said, her voice still strangled.

"Oh, I forgot to tell you J.T. said he was going over there to check things out," Eddie said.

Teddi followed her into the kitchen where Eddie started busily putting away groceries.

"Somebody wrote on the mirror in the living room with lipstick. They told me to get out of town," Teddi said.

Eddie paused. "You haven't been back long enough to make any enemies here. And you're the sister everyone likes anyway. I heard the teachers talking about how popular you are with the kids at school," she said.

"I know. I don't know what to make of it."

"Abner Wilson said that a stranger pulled into the gas station this morning asking about you. And Mrs. Nichols said somebody she'd never seen before came into the diner, and Mike Deaver said he thought he saw someone dressed in black skulking around the house last night."

"All that sounds like too many people in this town have been watching too much TV," Teddi said in a dry voice.

"Oh, come on. All the reports couldn't be coincidences," Eddie said.

"No. They're all merely products of overactive imaginations."

"Well then who broke in your house leaving sinister messages on your mirror?"

"I don't know," Teddi said with a sigh. She didn't want to believe all this was happening to her right as J.T. came back into her life. It was simply too much of a coincidence.

"Oh, no, where's J.T now?" Eddie exclaimed loudly, causing Teddi to jump and hit her head on one of the cabinets.

"Will you please cut the melodrama? He probably went to get a paper or something."

"All right, if you say so," Eddie said. "Anyway, you won't believe what happened to me last night."

Teddi waited, glad that Eddie was changing the subject back to her favorite topic, herself.

"Cecil called me. I was bored and I decided to let him have a taste, and he turned me down cold for the second time. I better not see his sorry rear again soon."

Teddi grinned. Good for Cecil. "It sounds like he didn't give you the chance to see it the first time," she said. "Are you coming to dinner tonight?"

"Not if Cecil's there," Eddie declared indignantly.

"You avoid him too hard, and he'll know that he got to you. And there's nothing a man likes better than to get to you, you know that?"

Eddie was silent for a moment. "Okay, I'll be there," she said. Teddi smiled to herself.

They heard the sound of a door opening. "There J.T. is now," Teddi said.

"What do you mean you're leaving? Did all that we said to each other, all that we promised mean nothing to you? How dare you?" Teddi's voice vibrated with anger.

"I can't risk it, baby. It's time to move on."

Teddi pulled back her arm and slapped him as hard as she could across the face. J.T.'s head snapped back from the blow, his eyes narrowed. Then he was still, too still. Teddi felt a pinch of fear. Had she gone too far?

Then the tense atmosphere snapped like a stepped-on twig.

"Lord, Teddi," J.T. said, rubbing his jaw. "Though I suppose I should be thankful you didn't shoot me."

Teddi dissolved into tears and J.T. pulled her into his arms.

"You need to understand," he started to say.

She pulled away. "*You* need to understand. People in this town are more excited than they've been in years. They're seeing spooks around every corner. That stuff about Wilkins seeing somebody bugging our house is a bunch of tripe. Wilkins couldn't see the nose on his face if he got a magnifying glass."

"Even so," J.T. said. "What about the message on the mirror? Someone wrote it after I left and before you came. The timing was too perfect, they must have been watching us."

"Even so, what? I'm a junior high school teacher. There are pranks all the time. Especially now, when they know I'm celebrating Kwanzaa and having guests. The bottom line is that you said we were a family, and we'd stick together no matter what. So why, when things get a little tough, do you want to cut and run?" Tears were running silent tracks down Teddi's cheeks. "Why do you want to leave us again?"

J.T. buried his face in her shoulder and inhaled. "I don't want to go anywhere, baby. I don't want to go anywhere."

Fifteen

At the bottom of education, at the bottom of politics, even at the bottom of religion, there must be economic independence.

—*Booker T. Washington*

Teddi's heart fluttered like moth wings and her breath came fast between her softly parted lips. Long minutes passed before the aftermath of J.T.'s loving ebbed from her body. She snuggled up to him, and he gave a little grunt of acknowledgment, but she could tell he was already settling into the deep, regular breathing of sleep.

Strong, bittersweet love swept between them, overflowing with tenderness, spiced with fear, and overlaid with a touch of Teddi's anger. Her sister always said that makin' up love was worth the fighting, and that must be so.

The solution to her dilemma was a simple one, she was never going to let J.T. go again. Never.

Teddi patted her head wrap as she placed the filled, fragrant dishes on the table. Her parents' house was filled to overflowing and the excited babble of voices reached her ears.

J.T. entertained Dixon's business leaders of color and their families while she finished setting out the food. An African-American farm supply owner, Mitchell Green, who ran the decades-old family business, was a fixture, and to the farmers around Dixon, the Green family had always offered the best values for the price. And that was what mattered to them. The Green business boomed, even though hardly any of its patrons were African-American.

Reverend Perry had come a second time to celebrate Kwanzaa with his partner Deacon Brown. They produced the best barbecue for miles around. Cecil Jennings, the bank vice president, and Timothy Harrel, a life insurance salesman, were present along with Taylor Reed, a Native American, who owned one of the two gas stations in town. Tony Ramirez, the owner of Ramirez Lawn Care rounded out her guest list.

Eddie soon sought out the refuge of the kitchen and Teddi. "All the wives are sitting in one corner, talking about Jerry Springer and soap operas. All the men are sitting in another corner talking about God-knows-what, and there must be a thousand kids running around like banshees."

"Sylvie is having a great time with the other children," Teddi said.

Eddie fanned herself with a hand carefully manicured with ice-blue nail polish to match her too tight and too short ice blue crushed velvet dress. "When I tried to join the men, you'd have thought I had propositioned one of them to do the nasty right there in the living room from how the wives looked at me," she said.

Teddi gave her a half grin. Eddie knew she looked good in that dress, but she also knew the dress was way too much for Dixon, Kansas, and the reverend's wife, Enid.

"Oh, my God!" Eddie exclaimed. Teddi looked at her in alarm.

"My nail polish is chipped," Eddie said holding up her hand and squinting at it with intense scrutiny. Teddi rolled her eyes.

"Cecil is being an idiot," Eddie announced.

"He seems to be treating you courteously. Even when you were so rude to him in front of everybody. Was that really necessary?" Teddi asked.

"I wasn't rude to him. I asked him a simple question, that's all."

"You handed him a jar of macadamia nuts with the top stuck on, and after giving him one second to try to remove it, you snatch it away with the comment, 'I guess you aren't man enough for this either.' So who is being the idiot?"

Eddie rolled her eyes, then focused on the buffet table.

"I don't know about this stuff. It smells good, but it doesn't quite look like food. You got some peanut butter in the pantry, I hope?"

"Don't change the subject," Teddi snapped. "And of all people, you should be open-minded about trying new things,"

"I am," Eddie rejoined. "Getting back to the subject, I'm going to try that new thing Cecil Jennings if it's the last thing I do."

"No point in warning you not to make a fool of yourself, or having a little self-respect, huh?"

Eddie tossed her head. "I got plenty of self-respect, sis." With an unladylike snort, she strode back into the living room.

Teddi looked after her with a slight smile. Why ever did she think she needed to worry about Cecil? The man had a little something about himself after all. He'd certainly got Eddie in a dither, and that was not an easy thing to do. Good for him.

The wives were scandalized when Teddi told them the ancient Ethiopians and Egyptians ate with their fingers. Teddi had to go back to the kitchen twice to get forks and knives. But once they'd tried the dishes, nobody complained about the food.

The plates on the buffet table were all scraped clean, except for a few spoonfuls of the salad, when J.T. lifted the unity cup to pour the libation. As he intoned the words to honor the ancestors, the atmosphere of the room changed. All the worry and fear seemed to dissipate. A tone of reverence descended; it was Kwanzaa again, a time to remember and reflect on the things that mattered most.

Sylvie lit the candles, and in the flickering light from the kinara, Teddi sat in the chair next to the Kwanzaa table.

"I'm going to speak to you about Madame C. J. Walker. She lived the Nguzo Saba of cooperative economics, and her life stands as a shining example of an African-American woman who made a difference," Teddi said.

"Sarah Breedlove was born in 1867, the daughter of slaves freed after the Civil War, in Delta Louisiana. She worked in the cotton fields with her family as a child. Her parents died in a yellow fever epidemic when she was seven and she was sent to Mississippi to live with her sister and brother-in-law.

"Her sister's husband abused her and she escaped him by marrying at fourteen. By the time Sarah was seventeen, she had a daughter, and at twenty, her husband was killed by a lynch mob and she was a widow.

"Then, Sarah and her daughter moved to St. Louis where she worked cleaning and cooking. She managed to support herself and her daughter and sent her daughter to school and on to college.

"In St. Louis, Sarah started to have trouble with hair loss. Back then, women twisted their hair and wrapped it in string to straighten out tight curls. This constant twisting and pulling was very hard on the hair. Sarah experimented with different oils and shampoos, and developed her Wonderful Hair Grower preparation, which helped her hair grow back in.

"She also invented the hot comb to straighten hair and improved her Hair Grower preparation, selling door to door with good success. In 1905, she moved to Denver with her sister-in-law and nieces and began full-fledged production of her hair products company. She married C. J. Walker in 1906, a journalist knowledge-able in advertising and mail-order sales. Expanding her operation, she appointed her daughter head of mail-order sales and started a sales force of black women, and by 1919 over 25,000 women were in business for themselves as Walker agents. One of her ads read: *Open your own shop; secure prosperity and freedom. Many women of all ages, confronted with the problem of earning a livelihood have mastered the Walker System.*

"Business boomed, and she opened beauty parlors across the country and colleges named after her daughter to train women in her method of hair grooming. In 1917, her business was the largest black-owned business in the country, started by a woman who could neither read nor write. Eventually she hired tutors to teach her, and lawyers and accountants to advise her, but she never loosed the helm until she died in 1919."

A fusillade of knocks sounded as Teddi ended her story. Justine opened the door. Bud's excited face was framed in the doorway.

"The word is out. I'm supposed to arrest J.T. The feds are coming in. If I were him, I'd clear out of town," he said.

The Fifth Day of Kwanzaa

The Nguzo Saba principle of the day is Nia (Purpose)
To make our collective vocation the building and developing of our community in order to restore our people to their traditional greatness.

The LORD shall preserve thy going out and thy coming in from this time forth, and even for evermore.
—*Psalm 121:8, The Holy Bible, King James Version*

Sixteen

Man is man because he is free to operate within the framework of his destiny. He is free to deliberate, to make decisions and to choose between alternatives.

—*Martin Luther King, Jr.*

"Mom, I know you'll take good care of Sylvie," Teddi said. Sylvie clung to her father, her eyes darting between her parents. J.T. knelt down in front of her. "I've got to go and finish something. I want you to remember that I'll always love you," he said.

Sylvie started to cry. "You're not coming back," she said. Teddi hugged her. "We'll both be back, baby. I need you to stay here and watch over Grandma and Grandpa."

Learning her mother was going also, seemed to calm Sylvie. J.T. started to open his mouth. "I'm going," Teddi said flatly.

He closed his mouth, sensing there was nothing else to say. Teddi was going with him and he couldn't stop her.

Eddie appeared with a duffel bag slung over her shoulder. "I'm going, too," she announced.

J.T. looked frustrated. "Why not pack up everybody in the house to go with us?" he asked, sarcasm barely evident in his voice.

"I could take a few days off work," Tony Ramirez said.

"As long as I'm back by Sunday," Reverend Perry added.

J.T. threw up his hands. "I was kidding," he said and stalked from the room.

Mitchell Green insisted they take his family's full-size conversion van. The van sported a kitchenette and a bathroom, everybody would travel comfortably.

Eddie raised an eyebrow as Teddi carried her Kwanzaa box to the van. "Why are you lugging that stuff? We're fugitives on the run."

"I'm going to finish celebrating Kwanzaa," Teddi said.

Eddie shrugged. "I don't know how you're going to manage that," she muttered under her breath.

"I'm going to manage," Teddi said, determination in her voice.

Justine hugged her daughter fiercely. "You hurry back now," she said.

J.T. kissed Sylvie goodbye, shook his father-in-law's hand, and climbed into the driver's seat of the conversion van.

Sylvie turned to Teddi, and her mother gathered her in her arms, feeling as if her heart would break. "You promise you're coming back?" she asked.

"Only the devil could keep me away from you," Teddi answered.

Sylvie grinned. "Daddy's tougher than the devil," was her answer. "You'll be back for sure."

J.T. leaned out of the window on the driver's side. "We need to go," he said.

Teddi gave Sylvie a final kiss and then they were on the road, with J.T.'s impatience barely controlled. Cecil sat next to J.T. in the front. He'd insisted on coming. Something about how another man would be useful, and anyway, he had a few days off work. Cecil could be surprisingly firm when he set his mind to something.

Teddi knew he'd ditch them at the first opportunity and go on by himself. She'd have to make sure that didn't happen. She wouldn't let him out of her sight.

Bud escorted them to Topeka. Teddi stared out the window at the featureless, black Kansas night. She missed Sylvie already, and sent a little prayer up for her, imagining her snug and safe tucked into her grandparents' bed.

The road rolled on, and Bud had turned back to Dixon on the outskirts of Topeka. A heavy feeling grew in the pit of Teddi's stomach as the comforting sight of the patrol car receded.

"So, where are we going?" asked Eddie brightly.

"Somewhere to drop all of you off," J.T. said.

"We're going to Ronnie's in Kansas City," Teddi said.

"Do you think that's safe?" Cecil asked.

"It'll be tomorrow before anybody discovers we're gone. Bud said the captain told the feds he wouldn't pick you up until daybreak," Teddi said.

"No. It's out of the question," J.T. said.

"C'mon, it sounds all right," Eddie said. "At least for a couple of days," she added.

"Yeah, let's go to Kansas City. It's an awfully big place. Nobody will find you there," added Cecil.

J.T. shook his head as he headed toward Kansas City. Teddi knew he planned to leave them at Ronnie's while he went on to New York. He planned wrong.

Eddie dropped the grocery bags on the counter. "I can't believe you're going to do all this cooking with all this going on," she said.

Teddi busied herself peering into bags and pulling items out to examine. "Cooking relaxes me, and the Lord knows I need relaxing," she said.

She'd taken over Stacy's kitchen. Ronnie's wife relinquished her territory with pleasure and voiced anticipation of Teddi's meal. Eddie realized Teddi's heart demanded the peace that the Kwanzaa ritual provided, and the food that went along with it.

J.T. would demand to be on the road by nightfall. She'd set her nieces and nephews to watching him, and as another precaution she had Ronnie disable every vehicle in the house, temporarily, of course. The distributor caps were all in a safe place.

Eddie peeked at Cecil. The romance novel she was reading wasn't holding her interest. Or was it that Cecil was so much more interesting? He was filling out a crossword puzzle. What was it with folks from Dixon and crossword puzzles? It seemed like they were always either doing one or just finished with one.

J.T. was pacing the room with pent-up nervous energy, probably wearing tracks in the carpet. Teddi was cooking a monstrous amount of food. Interesting how they all dealt with stress, Eddie thought.

She set the book aside, and moved close to Cecil. He looked up, faint alarm coloring his features. "Do you need some help?" she purred.

"Uhh, no," he said.

"I'd be happy to help, I'm so bored, and I love crossword puzzles."

At Eddie's words, J.T. stopped and dropped in a chair, watching them both with interest. "You hate crossword puzzles. You're always teasing Teddi about working them," he said to Eddie.

"Speaking of Teddi, why don't you go help her in the kitchen?" she snapped.

J.T. grinned, stood up, and stretched. "I guess I'll get

a beer. Want one, Cecil? You're going to need to cool off when Eddie gets through with you."

Cecil started to shake his head no, then thought better of it. "I'll join you," he said, following J.T. to the kitchen. He cast a nervous glance back at Eddie.

Eddie sucked her teeth. When they'd pulled into Ronnie's house last night, they were exhausted. Stacy separated Cecil and Eddie, with Eddie on a rollaway bed in the rec room in the basement and Cecil on the couch in the living room. Eddie had no chance to do the midnight creeping she planned. Ah, well, she'd have her chance later. Why would Cecil come with them anyway? One reason, and one reason only, he wanted to get next to her. He was nervous, that's all. She'd give him time. A little, anyway. She picked up her book, and settled back into the novel.

J.T. and Cecil had gotten their beer and then Teddi had shooed them out of the kitchen. She never liked men in the kitchen while she was cooking unless she put them to work. Something about their energy spoiled her rhythms. Cooking was like a heartbeat to her. Making food was her ritual, primal, basic, and womanly.

Last night she and J.T. slept in the guest bedroom. Exhaustion had removed any opportunity for them to talk before they fell asleep in tired, tangled heaps. J.T. had jumped out of bed in the morning, right as the sun was peeping over the horizon.

"Promise me something, J.T.," Teddi had asked.

J.T. looked startled. "I thought you were asleep," he'd said.

"Promise you'll never leave me again without saying goodbye."

Sadness touched J.T.'s features. "Baby, you know that it's not about what I want, it's about what's necessary."

"Promise me." Teddi's voice was low and fierce, tears tracking across her cheeks.

J.T. glanced at her out of the corner of his eye, defeat settling on his shoulders. Then, he took her in his arms.

"I promise," he said. "But I plan to be gone from here before nightfall. So you'd best speed up your plans for Kwanzaa."

Teddi chopped onions with unnecessary ferocity, tears stinging her eyes. She could hardly believe this was happening to her. Things like this happened to other people or in the movies. With all her heart she wished that she'd be back in Dixon, Kansas, with the family she loved by the end of the Kwanzaa holiday. A tear coursed down her cheek, and she wiped it with her sleeve. Darned onions, she thought, knowing the onions weren't the cause of her tears at all.

Seventeen

If you can only find it, there is a reason for everything.

—*Traditional saying*

The sports announcer's voice babbled excitedly
about another touchdown, and the roar of the crowd
blared from the television as Cecil's beeper went off for
what must have been the hundredth time.

"Who keeps beeping you, man?" J.T. asked.

Cecil didn't even bother to glance at it. "My ex-wife,"
he said.

J.T. chuckled. "No wonder you never look at the
thing. I wondered what was going on with that."

"I need to get rid of this beeper. I'm keeping it out
of habit."

"Why does your ex-wife beep you all the time? Especially since it appears you never call her back?" J.T.
asked.

"Because she's out of her mind. She took off with
another man last year, and frankly, I was relieved."

"That doesn't tell me why she's beeping you all the
time now."

"She thinks she wants me back. When she had me, she did exactly what she wanted to do, including partying, drinking too much, and stepping out with more than a few men, I suspect," Cecil said, sadness rather than anger appearing on his face.

"Why did you stay with her?"

"Habit, I suppose. We'd been together forever, and I felt it was up to me to look out for her. She had it real rough coming up." Cecil stared at the wedding band he still wore. "She didn't know how good she had it until she left. She's begging me to take her back. But I can't do it anymore."

J.T. shook his head, and they sat there in companionable silence while Cecil's beeper went off yet another time.

The sun was still high when Ronnie, Stacy, and their children sat along with Teddi and J.T. and Eddie and Cecil in front of the glowing light of the kinara, replete with the feast they'd just eaten.

"I have a story," Cecil said. Teddi looked at him in surprise.

"I want to tell the story of Cinque, who embodies the principle of purpose."

Teddi noticed Eddie edged closer to Cecil. Sis needed to give up on trying so hard, and let things unfold naturally. Cecil wouldn't be here if he wasn't interested in Eddie.

"When Cinque was about twenty-eight, he was ambushed and captured near his village," Cecil said. "Soon Cinque was forced into the hold of a ship to begin the terrible middle passage that thirty million Africans had traveled. He survived the trip and reached Havana, where he was fattened like a prize bull for the market. He was bought by a Spaniard who owned a sugar plantation in Haiti. He shared the cost to transport his slaves to Haiti with another slave owner aboard the ship the *Amistad.*

"Cinque picked the lock of his chains with a loose nail he'd pulled from a plank. Once free, he freed four fellow Africans. They opened a crate of cutlasses and armed themselves. Within seconds a fierce battle was going on and the slaves took the ship. The two Spanish owners locked themselves in the cabin.

"One of the slaveowner's servants spoke the same language as Cinque. Using the translator, Cinque offered a bargain, he would spare the slaveowner's lives in return for safe passage back to Africa. The slaveowners agreed.

"During the day they sailed toward Africa but at night they turned back West, with their valuable cargo. They were poor navigators and they failed to return to Cuba like they'd schemed.

"They finally anchored at Montauk Point on the eastern tip of Long Island, New York. The townspeople were surprised when a group of nearly naked Africans marched into their town holding Spanish gold. While Cinque was in town, the ship was boarded by the U.S. military and the Africans surrendered.

"The slaveowner demanded that the slaves be turned over to him at once, but the captain of the ship that had taken the *Amistad* also set claim to the ship and its human cargo. Cinque and the Africans were imprisoned until the matter went to court.

"The *Amistad* incident became highly publicized and a lawyer and translator was procured for Cinque and his fellow Africans. In the courtroom, Cinque gave one of the few eyewitness accounts on record of the horrors of the "middle passage" from Africa.

"Finally, Cinque turned to the judge and said in English, 'Give . . . us . . . free!'

"Cinque was freed to the custody of the President of the United States. At that time, Martin Van Buren courted the wealthy southern landowners and the case was appealed until it reached the Supreme Court. John Quincy Adams argued the case before the justices and Cinque was freed. He stayed in the United States for another year and lectured and traveled on behalf of abolitionist groups.

"When he returned to Africa, his wife and children were gone, likely victims of slavers. Cinque started a new family and died at the age of sixty-eight.

"His name stands for the millions of slaves that made the middle passage and held the memories of their homeland Africa in their hearts. Cinque was one of the very few who had the purpose and the good fortune to find freedom at the end of his long journey."

Four hours down the highway heading east, J.T. finally allowed them a rest break.

Teddi shivered in the cold while the operator quizzed her mother whether she would accept a collect call.

"Mama, I'm okay, but I only have a few minutes. Can I speak with Sylvie?"

She waited impatiently until she heard Sylvie's voice on the phone.

"I miss you, baby," she said, cradling the receiver.

"I miss you and Daddy, too. When are you going to be back?"

"Real soon," she said, praying that it was the truth.

That call didn't make her feel better, only intensified her longing for her daughter. Then, she remembered

Stacy had extracted a promise that she call and let her sister-in-law know they were all right.

Stacy picked up the phone on the first ring. "Thank God you called," she said breathlessly. "Federal agents were just here asking questions about you."

Eighteen

I had reasoned dis out in my mind; there was one of two things I had a right to, liberty or death; if I could not have one, I would have the other, for no man should take me alive; I should fight for my liberty as long as my strength lasted, and when the time came for me to go, the Lord would let them take me.

—*Harriet Tubman*

Another city, an anonymous motel room. Teddi tossed with restless dreams of slamming car doors and steps receding into the distance. Something about those sounds meant loss and abandonment to her. In actuality it was the too thin walls of the motel and the comings and goings of the guests that disturbed her sleep. Still, slamming car doors were symbolic. The sound signified getting out, leaving, walking away.

She opened her eyes in the dark room, a half formed thought, more a fear really, struck her. She was alone in the bed. Coming suddenly to full wakefulness, she bolted upright. Oh, God, was J.T. gone? Then she saw his figure huddled near the opposite end of the bed instead of wrapped around her as was his habit. She slowly exhaled relief.

He'd tripped when she told him that Stacy had said federal agents had come looking for them. "I need to move," he'd said. "And I need to move alone. I've got to stop playing games, baby. This is for real, and I'm not going to let them take me."

There was nothing she could say. Teddi hated feeling helpless most of all. Her life was careening like a roller coaster gone amuck and she was powerless to switch on the brakes. She couldn't control J.T. He'd walk away despite the loving. And the rotten thing about it was J.T.'s defection wouldn't kill her love for him, only make it hurt. If he walked away now, it would be the last time she would see him and feel her soul mate next to her. Her very bones knew it. How could she be so blessed with love and yet so cursed?

They were on the run with the law and worse after them on the last day of the old year. Depression and defeat threatened her with black clouds of fear and doubt. Then a thought cut through her melancholy like a bright silvery ray; thought creates triumph.

Thought creates triumph? Where did that come from? A glimmer of an idea came into being. The idea was daring, bold, and decisive, this was no time for hesitation, half-measures, and doubt. First came thought, then action to create the reality she chose.

With sudden decision, Teddi threw off the covers and leaned over, reaching for J.T.'s laptop. She cast a glance at him to make sure he was asleep and crept silently to the bathroom.

Sitting on the cold, hard seat of the lid of the toilet, she opened J.T.'s laptop and booted up. The time on the computer screen read 2:00 A.M. Ah, there it was, his plans to get the information Paul left. She frantically worked through sequences of letters and numbers, searching for the password to open the file, with no luck. Teddi bit her lip.

She was about ready to give up in defeat when she typed her own name into the password query box. To her surprise, the file opened. She leaned forward to read, drawing in a breath between her teeth. So he planned to leave tomorrow morning, and do it on a holiday. Smart, there'd be fewer people around.

He'd researched the cleaning crew that would be in after the annual New Year's party. J.T.'s plan clicked into place, and the beginning glimmers of her own plan took form. She nodded to herself. Teddi's eyes narrowed as she memorized the necessary information.

When she was finished, she carefully placed the laptop back exactly where she found it. J.T. was tossing and muttering in his sleep. She slid in next to him and was startled at the heat that radiated from his body. Teddi laid her hand lightly on his forehead. Oh, no, he was burning up.

She turned on the lamp next to the bed and rummaged through the backpack he'd brought until she found acetaminophen. Pouring him a glass of water in the flimsy clear plastic cups the motel provided, she gently nudged him awake.

"Here, take this," she said. "You've got a fever."

J.T. sat up in bed, bleary eyed, and swallowed the pills without a word. He flopped back down and buried himself back under the covers.

"Not so soon," Teddi said. "I want to look at that leg." She'd almost forgotten about his wound the past few days. J.T. didn't complain, and so much had been happening. He made a sound of protest, but she could see that he didn't feel good enough to put up much resistance.

She pulled off the bandage. His wound didn't look bad at all, it was almost healed.

"I told you it wasn't the leg. I probably have a twenty-four-hour bug. If I could get some rest, I'll be fine tomorrow, J.T. said meaningfully.

"Let me get you some more fluids," Teddi said.

"No. Please, baby, turn off the lights and let me go back to sleep."

Teddi turned off the lamp, but sleep was a long time coming for her.

Eddie tossed and turned, also, but her frustrations were of a different nature. She'd never met a man she couldn't get, at least physically, and Cecil was frustrating the hell out of her. In the back of her mind, she realized that it was becoming less of a game to her.

She was wanting him for real and for reasons that were foreign to her. Not that he excited her, not that he was a "catch," not even that he was such a challenge, but that he was so real and genuinely nice. She wanted Cecil because he worked hard and held small-town values. Usually she judged men by the amount of money they made, and by the value of their car and other toys. She must be losing her mind. Cecil drove a Chevy Cavalier, for God's sake.

It didn't matter how much or why she wanted him, because he was blocking her overtures with the ease of a hockey goalie. She thought she had him for sure when he volunteered to accompany them as they fled across the country, but he hadn't given up a thing. Right about now, she'd love to have J.T. kill him. At least torture him a little. Because the Lord knew Cecil Jennings was torturing her.

Well, she'd had enough. It was time to take serious action. Eddie flung the covers off her and stalked into the bathroom. Fifteen minutes later, showered and perfumed with her best hot pink lingerie in place, she gave

a determined fluff of her hair. Hadn't she read somewhere that men's hormone levels were highest in the
early morning? With that thought, she marched over
and knocked on the door of Cecil's room.

Eddie's eyes widened at the sight of Cecil clad only
in pajama bottoms and a yawn. She pushed past him
into the darkened room and sat on the edge of the
tousled bed, sniffing loudly.

"I'm frightened, Cecil. I had the most dreadful
dream. The police caught us and we all went to jail,
and there was you and this big, bad man and . . . well,
you know."

Then she squinted as Cecil flipped the switch and
bright light flooded the room. "No, I don't know about
me and any big, bad man," he said. "But since you're
upset, I'll go get Teddi."

"That's not necessary," Eddie said quickly. "I don't
want Teddi, I want you." She let the edge of her pei-
gnoir fall open revealing the matching lace bra and
panty set underneath.

Cecil's eyebrows shot up. "I'd better run over to
McDonald's and get us some coffee and breakfast," he
said, stammering slightly.

"I'm not hungry," Eddie started to say, but Cecil had
already snatched his jeans and sweatshirt from the floor
and the bathroom door closed behind him.

Eddie gave a little cat's smile of satisfaction. Things
hadn't turned out exactly how she wanted, but the man
was rattled. Now onward to Plan B. She stretched out
languorously on the bed and awaited for Cecil to
emerge.

A few minutes later, Cecil opened the bathroom door
gingerly. "Come on out," Eddie called. "I won't bite . . .
unless you want me to," she said with a throaty chuckle.

Cecil emerged looking like a deer caught in headlights. "Sit down here and talk to me," Eddie patted the bed next to her.

Cecil swallowed hard. "I'm really hungry. I need to go and find something to eat."

Eddie stood up in a smooth motion and moved too close to him. She leaned forward, her lips almost touching his ear. "It's five A.M., nothing's open yet," she whispered. " 'Cept me," she added, her tongue darting out to moisten her lips.

Cecil choked. "There's a Quik Trip on the corner, it's open now," he stammered, backing away. Eddie muttered a curse as he fled, the door shutting behind him.

The Sixth Day of Kwanzaa

The Nguzo Saba principle of the day is *KUUMBA*
(Creativity)
To do always as much as we can, in whatever way we
can, in order to leave our community more beautiful
and beneficial than we inherited it.

The great I AM took the soul of the world and
wrapped some flesh around it and that made you.
—*Zora Neale Hurston*

Nineteen

Potential powers of creativity are within us and we have the duty to work assiduously to discover these powers.

—*Martin Luther King, Jr.*

The glow of the candles were ghostly in the stark motel room. Teddi watched J.T. as he sipped a glass of wine.

"I hope Sylvie is enjoying the Karamu," he said.

"I'm sure she is," Cecil answered.

They were a sober group for such a festive time. Tonight was the night of the largest and most festive Kwanzaa celebration, the Karamu feast. Teddi knew her mother was carrying on for her, making sure the celebration and potluck at the community center went smoothly, but she was missing it all so much.

She remembered the Karamu celebration she'd attended with J.T. and Sylvie three years ago. She took a dish to a friend's party in New York. There'd been drums, African dancers, and professional storytellers, with the most amazing amount and variety of foods and people. They'd had the best time and vowed to do it again next year. J.T. said they'd rent a place and have the party themselves if their friend didn't do it the next year. But when the next year came, her family was shattered and there was no Karamu. And this year they were on the run, separated from their child.

Her husband was dozing over his glass of wine. Cecil seemed to be engrossed in staring at his shoes and even Eddie had nothing to say. Determination replaced Teddi's depression as she lifted a slice of carry-out pizza to her lips and chewed. At least she had food, and her family was intact. Now she had a plan. She watched J.T. through narrowed eyes.

"Baby, you're looking at me like I'm a slice of sweet potato pie," J.T. said to Teddi.

Eddie laughed. "Right about now, I wish you were. One of Teddi's sweet potato pies with whipped cream, after we finished chowing on the glazed ham, black-eyed peas, collard greens, and chitlins."

"Yes, Lord," said Cecil fervently.

"I'd be cooking those things for tomorrow, I was going to take West African food to the Karamu tonight," Teddi said.

"What were you going to take?" J.T. asked.

"Dakar fish, akara balls, and West African coconut pie," Teddi answered.

"Uh, uh, uh. Here we are on the run, and the folks are partying and eating good at the community center in Dixon, and it was all your idea, Teddi. Just doesn't seem fair," Eddie said.

"Whole lot of things don't seem fair," Teddi answered, staring into the light of the black candle.

"Sure don't," Eddie said, looking at Cecil and frowning. Cecil looked away.

"Sometimes I wonder about folk who turn down good dishes like Teddi cooks," Eddie continued. "Sometimes people don't prefer good home cooking, they prefer different things." Eddie stared at Cecil. "Not saying anything is wrong with preferring different things, as long as you're totally honest about your preferences."

"What are you talking about?" J.T. asked.

"Cecil knows what I'm talking about," Eddie answered.

"No, I don't," Cecil said. He looked at Eddie. "You remind me of Sally, my ex-wife," he added.

Why did he have to go there? Teddi thought.

"Oh, nooo, excuse me," Eddie said. "I am nothing like that wench Sally, and I don't appreciate being compared to her."

"Don't call her a wench," Teddi said.

"You stay out of it, I can call that wench anything I want to," Eddie snapped.

"Yeah, you'd better stay out of it, Teddi," J.T. said, looking uncomfortable.

Teddi shot him a murderous glance.

"What story were you going to tell tonight?" Cecil asked, desperately trying to change the subject.

"Yeah, lighten things up, baby," J.T. said.

Teddi fidgeted, she wasn't in the mood for a story. "I was going to tell you about Zora Neale Hurston, who lived the principle of creativity."

Eddie lifted her glass and poured a tiny puddle of wine on the carpet. "Hail, Zora," she said. "C'mon Teddi, tell us who this Zora is? Or was . . . I know she got to be someone dead if you planned to talk about her on Kwanzaa."

Cecil nodded. "Tell us the story."

So Teddi took a deep breath and began.

"Zora Neale Hurston was a writer, and you're right Eddie, she's dead. She died in 1960, poor and alone in a welfare home after sixty-nine years of living large, loving life, and listening and learning about the stories people tell. She left behind her thoughts, opinions, and experiences crystallized and frozen in her writings. Zora was the most published black woman of her time.

"Growing up in Eatonville, Florida, she had a happy childhood until her mother died when she was nine. She worked as a maid until she enrolled in school in Baltimore. Zora loved to learn, and after she graduated high school, she enrolled in Howard University. This is where she started to write. Her first story was published in Howard University's literary magazine.

"She won a scholarship to Barnard College in New York, and became the school's first black student. There she became involved with the Harlem Renaissance writers, and became successful with her writing.

"After she graduated from Barnard, she studied anthropology at Columbia University. For the next ten years Zora researched and collected lore and folktales from African-American people. She studied and researched the voodoo religion more than any other anthropologist, while she traveled widely and cultivated friendships with writers and other creative people of her time, such as Langston Hughes.

"She was criticized frequently for writing about the richness of African-American culture and the joys of life rather than the poverty, misery, and racism with which most African-Americans lived. By the late '40s she had trouble getting her books and articles published. Money trouble always chased her and caught her in the end.

"Zora's power was in her prose, the turn of her phrase, and the magic of her words. She never stopped creating and through her creations, her voice lives, and so does her memory."

When Teddi finished, she watched J.T. His eyes were closed and his breathing deep and regular. She turned to Cecil and Eddie. "The drug I put in his wine worked. He's out. Help me get him to bed and tie him up."

Cecil's features turned grim, but he nodded and together they struggled to get J.T.'s heavy figure in the bed.

Twenty

If you run into a wall, don't turn around and give up. Figure out how to climb it, go through it, or work around it.

—*Michael Jordan*

"Unbelievable. You people must be out of your freaking minds. Untie me, now!" J.T.'s voice rose to a roar and Eddie flinched. Cecil shook his head calmly. Eddie wondered how Cecil stayed so cool with J.T. glaring pure murder at him.

Eddie had no idea Cecil could be so bossy. He'd taken charge of everything, staying with J.T. all night, sending her out to get them coffee and breakfast.

"Teddi said to leave you be until she gets back. If you have to go to the bathroom I can help," Cecil said.

The look J.T. shot at him should have withered him on the spot. "Where is Teddi?" J.T. ground out.

"She went to New York to retrieve the information Paul left," Eddie said.

If the air could smoke, it would have with the string of curses J.T. let loose.

"She said you were sick. She said that the plan would have a much greater chance of success if she pulled it off. Teddi made sense. If everything goes well, she'll be back this evening," Cecil offered.

J.T. squinted at Cecil as if planning his slow, torturous demise, which if J.T. had anything to do with it, would be soon.

Eddie shifted from foot to foot. "I'm going out," she announced. "I hear some good New Year's Day sales are going on." She nervously glanced at J.T. His eyes hadn't moved from Cecil. It was as if she wasn't there. "You want anything, J.T.?"

Silence. Well, she'd leave them at their stare-down. It must be a man-thing. Eddie gave them both a cheery wave as she walked out the door.

Teddi thought she'd been lonely after J.T. left, but that was nothing compared with how she felt now. Dark nothingness echoed within her, like the night sky, and she'd give almost anything to feel J.T.'s arms around her. Is this how he'd felt the past two years? She didn't know how he'd endured it. But he had, and now she would make sure they all stayed safe. Teddi never bought into the macho belief that as the wife she needed the protection.

She'd always felt undeniably strong in her womanhood. Even at the worst times there was never any doubt that she'd go on and raise Sylvie without either of them knowing want. Do what you got to do. Black women had lived by those words for centuries. It never did get much easier, just more certain. Teddi would do what she had to do. Because, without a doubt, her man would get himself killed doing it, and she and Sylvie needed him too much.

It was a simple thing. Why, she'd be back in Chicago by nightfall. She'd taken a taxi to the airport, and bought a ticket under an assumed name with the cash she had lifted out of J.T.'s duffel bag. She didn't have a problem getting a flight on the evening of New Year's Eve, and she was airborne by 9 P.M.

She leaned back in her seat and pictured Sylvie. One of Sylvie's favorite stories was an Ethiopian folktale about a boy named Mammo. He wasn't a very bright boy, but he was obedient and tried to do what his mother wanted. He kept doing it wrong, but in spite of this, everything turned out well for Mammo. She and Sylvie had a long conversation over what Kwanzaa principle this story illustrated. They'd decided on purpose and Sylvie had practiced the story to tell on the fifth day of Kwanzaa. She'd missed hearing the tale, and the longing for her daughter's presence became an ache.

She had to get the information to exonerate J.T. by the time the sun set again. She had a one-time shot at it, and it was unthinkable that she fail. They'd all be home together in Dixon, Kansas, to share the evening meal and celebrate the seventh day of Kwanzaa, she thought with the intensity and power of a prayer. It had to be so.

The fasten seat belt sign came on with a chime. They were getting ready to land at Kennedy. Teddi's hands trembled as she fumbled with her seat belt, but she refused to acknowledge fear. Only her strength existed.

Her ears felt full from the plane's rapid descent, and instead of falling into the pool of fear by thinking about what she had to do, Teddi quieted her mind and closed her eyes, concentrating on her breath. In and out. The bump of the airplane's wheels on the tarmac, and they were there. She landed back in New York City, coming full circle.

Eddie sighed as she looked at herself in the mirror of the upscale lingerie store. The gold lace looked good against her bronze skin, classier than the hot pink set she'd tried and failed to wow Cecil with. Why couldn't she get this dorky guy from Kansas in bed? In her heart, she didn't believe he was gay.

She sighed again, the question was, why was she trying so hard? What was it about Cecil that made her want him so bad? Maybe she was going after him all wrong, maybe he liked a quieter, softer beauty. He had nerve saying she reminded him of his ex-wife. She'd never gotten along with that heifer. Maybe she should change, not speak her mind so freely.

Get a grip, Eddie, she told herself. Self-doubt was not what she was about. Confidence made the girl. She was who she was, period, and if Cecil didn't like it . . .

Eddie fluffed her hair and thought about what happened last night. Before Cecil walked away from her, she saw in his eyes how much he wanted her. She knew it without a doubt. So, she'd back off and let him play whatever game he had in mind, so long as in the end, she'd have him. That was all she needed, and she was positive one good round of the nasty was all it would take to get Cecil Jennings out of her system. It'd better be.

She'd get the gold, and the creme set, too. Maybe it was time she added some pastels to her nighttime wardrobe.

Both men jumped when Eddie let herself into the motel room. Cecil had untied the pantyhose he used to tie J.T.'s wrists and they were playing cards, with fast food bags and styrofoam boxes scattered around. The taxi cab driver followed her laden with packages.

The taxi driver's eyes widened when he saw J.T.'s ankles wrapped with pantyhose.

"They're just playing one of their favorite games,"

Eddie whispered to the driver as she proffered a tip. The driver's eyebrows shot up and he hastily exited.

J.T. had a faintly amused expression on his face at Cecil's obvious dismay at his cards.

Eddie draped herself over Cecil's shoulder as she examined his hand. "I hope you know when to fold 'em," she said. "Because those cards are hurting you bad."

Cecil started to smile and reach out to her, but then he caught himself and lowered his head to his cards.

Eddie's lips curved. It was only a matter of time, she thought.

J.T. was staring at the mound of Eddie's purchases. "I hope you used cash," he said.

"Please. I don't carry that much cash on me," she answered.

J.T. frowned. "We've got to leave now," he said to Cecil.

"Why?"

"Her credit cards will be traced. In a short amount of time they'll pinpoint our location. We've got to get out of here now."

It was close to midnight when Teddi landed in New York. New Year's festivity was in the air, and accentuated her feelings of loneliness and isolation. She walked toward the line of parked taxis. It was important she chose well.

She got into a taxi driven by a middle-aged man, his face sprinkled with a salt and pepper beard. His dark skin was almost the exact same shade as J.T.'s, but it was his eyes that made her choose him. They were sad, bright, knowing, and above all, kind.

"Where you want to go, lady?" the taxi driver asked. Teddi hesitated and he pulled away from the curb.

"Terrible night to be alone isn't it?" he asked.

She nodded and the driver's eyes met hers in the back mirror. "Yes. Yes, it's a hard night to be alone," she said. "I want to go to an all-night supermarket," she added.

Asking the driver to wait, she bought cleaning supplies, a basket to carry them in, a feather duster, a bandanna, and an apron. She hesitated, then threw a bottle of sparkling grape juice and a package of fluted plastic champagne glasses in the shopping cart.

"Do you know a place where there's a good view of the river?" Teddi asked.

He parked on a hill. Teddi moved to the front seat and poured the grape juice.

"My wife left me last year," the taxi driver said. "Not that it makes much difference. I always worked the holidays anyway."

He paused and took a sip. "It's funny, it never was as lonely when I knew she'd be home waiting for me."

"My husband left me two years ago."

"Tough luck, huh?"

"He just came back. That's what's getting me through, knowing he's waiting for me."

"This stuff is really good," the taxi driver said, holding out his glass for a refill. "So why aren't you with him then?"

"It's a long story," Teddi answered. "It all comes down to something I have to do. Something that has to be done tonight."

Teddi shot a glance under her lashes at the taxi driver. "Will you help me?" she asked, and dropped a hundred dollar bill in his lap.

He gently picked up the bill and handed it back to her. "I don't need your money."

Teddi bit her lip, disappointed. What was she going to do now?

"Lady, I'm going to help you," he continued. "But I

won't take your money. Seems like we're both kinda lost tonight. Kindred spirits I guess. If I do a good deed, maybe something will go right with me for a change."

Teddi gazed at the moonlight gleaming on the river. "Maybe it will at that," she said. And at that moment, fireworks exploded over the Hudson to herald the coming year.

Sylvie's favorite story about Mammo the Fool, An Ethiopian Folktale

Mammo was the only son of a poor woman who made her living selling injera, a thin Ethiopian flat bread, and teffa, barley beer. She was always mad at her son Mammo because he was so foolish. Whenever Mammo's mommy sent him out on an errand, the other village children would gather and shout at him, "Fool! Fool!" Mammo didn't mind, he'd stop and shout and laugh with them, forgetting all about the errand his mother sent him on.

One day she sent him to the market to buy butter. The butter was in a cup and Mammo was carrying the cup in his hands when a boy shouted at him, "Mammo, why are you holding the butter that way? Throw away the cup and put it on your head! That's how you're supposed to carry it."

Mammo thought about it for a second, and put the lump of butter on his head. The sun was high and very hot, and soon the butter melted and ran down his face. When he got home empty handed, his mommy was mad. When Mammo told her what happened to the butter, she spanked him.

"You should have carried the butter in you hands, not on your head," she said.

The next day she sent Mammo to fetch a cat from a neighbor's house. So off he went. Mammo remembered

what his mommy had said so he was sure to hold the
cat very tightly in his hands. The poor cat struggled
and hissed and spit and scratched Mammo all up and
he had to let the cat go.

When he got home he had no cat and scratched up
fingers. His mommy was mad and spanked him again.
She said, "You should have pulled the cat along at the
end of a string."

A few days later Mammo's mommy sent him to the
butcher's for some meat. When he got the meat he remembered to tie a string to it and drag it down the
road like his mommy had told him. He didn't want to
get into trouble like he had for not dragging the cat.

Soon, all the village children were following him,
laughing and shouting at Mammo. The dogs in the
village came running when they smelled the meat.
Mammo was happy he was finally doing something
right.

When he got home he proudly pulled the meat in
front of him to give to his mommy. But there was no
meat left, only a little piece of bone attached to the
string. Boy, did he get a big spanking then. "Why did
you drag the meat?" his mommy cried. "You should
have carried it on your back!"

The next week, Mammo's mommy told him to take
the donkey out to the field. Mammo remembered his
mommy's advice and with all his strength heaved the
donkey on his back and started down the road.

A young girl was watching Mammo from her window,
and when she saw him with the donkey on his back,
she began to laugh. She laughed so hard she almost
fell over. Her parents rushed into the room, and they
heard her say, "Look at that fool with the donkey on
his back!"

The parents were surprised and overjoyed to hear
their daughter laugh because she had a terrible illness.

She hadn't been able to smile or laugh for seven years.
The father was so happy, he ran out and got Mammo
and introduced him to his daughter. Mammo was shy
and looked at his feet, but the daughter smiled slowly
and nodded. So the father gave Mammo his daughter's
hand in marriage.

Now Mammo was Prince Mammo, because the
daughter was a beautiful princess. And they lived happily ever after all because Mammo kept trying to do
what he was supposed to do.

The Seventh Day of Kwanzaa

The Nguzo Saba of the day is the principle of *IMANI*
(Faith)
To believe with all our hearts in our people, our parents, our teachers, our leaders, and in the righteousness and victory of our struggle.

Before the ship of your life reaches its last harbor, there will be long drawn-out storms, howling and jostling winds, and the tempestuous sea that make the heart stand still. If you do not have a deep and patient faith in God, you will be powerless to face the delay, disappointment and vicissitudes that inevitably come.

—*Martin Luther King, Jr.*

Twenty-one

Faith is the flip side of fear.

—*Susan Taylor*

It was barely noon and Eddie was stuffing her purchases into suitcases when she heard cars pull up in front of the motel. She heard doors slam, and approaching footsteps. Oh Lord, it couldn't be. She drew her curtain to the side and peeked out.

"Open up, police," one of the men called outside of Cecil's door.

She thought her heart would stop. J.T. and Cecil were next door in the room Teddi and J.T. shared. How could they make a break for it with all those men in black standing around?

She cast a despairing look at her new purchases. She had the keys to the van. She'd have to book. Her hope was that they would have no idea what room she was in, since they registered under assumed names, or a good idea what she looked like. She quickly wrapped her hair up in a scarf, and drew on her rattiest pair of jeans, and a pair of oversized sunglasses. She grabbed her purse and walked out of her hotel room as nonchalantly as she could, going in the opposite direction from the room Cecil and J.T. were in. Thank God J.T. had parked the van around the corner, out of sight.

"Open up or we're coming in," she heard the man outside J.T.'s room call. They drew guns and stood at the sides. Teddi would kill her if she let J.T. get shot Eddie thought. She didn't even want to think about how she'd feel if Cecil got hurt. She quickly got into the van and started it up, pulling it out of the parking space, but still out of sight of the police.

She heard the police burst into the door. At that moment she revved up the van and careened around the corner to their room. Cecil and J.T. came out of a different room and ran toward the van.

"Get in," she screamed. They jumped into the side door she'd left open and she peeled out of the parking lot.

It seemed like two seconds later she heard the sound of sirens behind her. "Jesus, they're shooting at us," Eddie screamed.

"Just drive," J.T. yelled back. "Go toward Lake Shore Drive, toward the traffic."

"There is a game at the stadium today, we'll be stuck and they'll get us."

"No, it's our best chance. We need to ditch the van."

Glass exploded inward as the rear window of the van was shot out and Cecil yelled.

Eddie put her foot on the gas and moved. These car chases looked easier on TV than they were for real. She was about to have a heart attack.

Suddenly, they hit a solid wall of traffic, fans leaving the football game.

"Let's go," Cecil said. They spilled out of the car, running across the cars at a standstill.

They ran to a parking lot near the stadium overfilled with vehicles.

"Keep down," J.T. said. "That's the one," he said,

indicating a black Ford Bronco. He took out a slim-jim from the backpack he carried and within seconds the car was open.

"I'm not running from the police in a Ford Bronco," Eddie declared. "We'll be no better off than O.J.—"

"Get in," Cecil said, pushing her into the vehicle.

"Keep your heads down," J.T. said, and fumbled under the dashboard.

It sounded like police sirens were all around them.

"We're stealing a car," Eddie said. "I can't believe we're stealing a car."

"We're just borrowing it," J.T. said, and with those words the motor finally started. "Get in the front with me, Eddie. Cecil, keep your head down."

They pulled slowly out of the parking lot and turned opposite to the to the direction of the traffic, toward the heart of the city, Chicago.

That was when Eddie noticed the dark maroon blood shading Cecil's shirt. "Omigod!" she exclaimed. "You've been shot."

The party was still in full swing at the building where J.T. used to work. Every year of their marriage they'd attended the annual New Year's Eve party. This was the first time she was going alone.

"Thank you," she said to the taxi driver. He nodded and pressed her hand. "You be real careful in there. I know your husband wants you back in one piece, you're a special one."

She watched as the taxi driver pulled off, then tied the bandanna around her head. She reached for her basket of cleaning supplies and climbed the steps into the building foyer.

Three security guards had an open bottle of champagne out, and a woman was draped across one of their laps. She nodded to them as she passed. They didn't even notice her. She entered the bathrooms and started cleaning. Slowly she made her way toward the offices. The baleful eye of a security video looked at her, and a locked door that only a magnetic key and codes could open blocked her way to the computers and phone lines. That was not the way she was going to get in.

Laughter sounded down the hall, and Teddi hid out of sight around a corner. A couple approached, wrapped around each other, whispering and giggling in each other's ears.

"This way," the man said fumbling in his wallet for his card. He found it and inserted it into the slot and pressed in the code.

"Yes," the woman moaned, rubbing herself against him.

They stumbled through the door, and Teddi followed swiftly, grabbing the door before it closed. She cast an eye over her shoulder at the security monitor. No one was watching tonight, and when they reviewed the tapes it would be too late.

"My boss's desk is over here," Teddi heard the man say. She went in the opposite direction, and slipped behind one of the computer monitors. Her fingers flew as she input the information she'd memorized.

It took a while, but there it was, the information Paul left. She sent a silent prayer of thanks, and slipped in a disk.

"What's this?" the man said, the blue light of the computer screen reflecting off his face. "Someone's downloading information from the main frame."

An older blond woman approached behind him. "Is anybody authorized to be working tonight?"

"No, but it's likely nothing. The party's going on, and

I'd bet somebody couldn't resist doing it on the boss's desk. Now, they're probably just playing around with the computer."

The blond frowned. "All those desks belong to me." She tapped a perfectly manicured finger on the desk. "Get down there and see about it."

He hesitated, "For goodness sakes, Theresa, it's New Year's," he said.

She arched a brow. "Now," she said.

"Oh, Cecil, Cecil, hold on," Eddie wailed.

"I'm all right," Cecil answered, looking embarrassed.

"Why didn't you say something?" J.T. asked.

"Everybody was pretty preoccupied."

J.T. looked at him carefully, noting his pallor, his quick, rapid breaths, and the tiny beads of cold sweat erupting on his brow. "We need to get you to a hospital, man," he said.

"It's really not that bad," he said again.

"Are you sure you're going to be all right for a while longer? I planned to take a train out of here," J.T. said.

"I'll be fine. Let's get you out of this area first," Cecil said.

"Are you sure? I can go with you to the hospital," Eddie said.

"No, I want to get on the train like J.T. planned, then I may take you up on your offer," Cecil said.

Eddie squeezed his hand. "I'm counting on that," she said, as they maneuvered the Bronco through the crowded downtown streets.

Twenty-two

They seemed to be staring at the dark, but their eyes
were watching God.

—*Zora Neale Hurston*

Eddie let Cecil lean on her, holding him tight like
a lover. They'd changed trains until J.T. was satisfied
they'd eluded detection. Cecil's steps steadily grew
more hesitant and his breath came in pants. When
they finally reached an empty seat, he sat down heavily
with his eyes closed and his skin ashen.

"We've got to get him to a hospital," Eddie whispered
to J.T., who sat in front of them.

"I never should have let him get on the el," J.T. replied, looking grim.

"Cecil are you sure you're okay?" she asked. There
was no reply. Then his eyes opened slowly.

"It is starting to get a little tough to breathe," he
finally gasped. "Maybe you should drop me off at a
hospital pretty soon."

Teddi looked around for a way out other than the
door the security camera was trained on. She could find

nothing but blind corridors and windows that didn't
open. The moans and gasps from the office down the
hall grew louder and louder, then subsided. Her instincts were telling her to get out of here before that
couple got up and started looking around for a bathroom.

Teddi got her cleaning supplies and slipped out of
the door, trying to ignore the baleful eye of the security
camera. She casually walked past the security desk toward the front entrance. Only one security guard was
now present and he was hanging up the phone.
"Ma'am," he called, "Ma'am, I need to speak to you."

Adrenalin poured through her, and she dropped the
basket of cleaning supplies and bolted. A group of
guests stood by the way out the front entrance. She took
off down a side corridor, hearing the footfalls of the
security guard as he came up behind her.

He caught her and spun her around. He found himself looking down the barrel of a gun. "Back off mister,
I will use this," Teddi said.

"I think not," said a voice from behind her. She
looked over her shoulder, a tall, slim man in a dark suit
had a gun trained on her. She could tell by his stance
and the look in his eye that he wouldn't hesitate to use
his weapon either. Teddi lowered the taxi driver's gun
in defeat.

The Cook County Hospital emergency room reception area looked like a war zone.

"Happy New Year's Day," J.T. said wryly, observing
the room full of the ill and injured.

Eddie gave up trying to get the attention of the har-
ried nurses at the reception desk. She walked back into
the treatment area and searched for Cecil's name on

the large board that listed the patient name, treatment area, nurse, resident, and complaint.

A young man was writing John Doe, gunshot wound, on the board.

"The guy that just came in with the gunshot? Where is he?" Eddie asked.

"He's going to surgery," he said.

With a stifled sob, Eddie turned to leave and ran right into J.T.'s hard arms. He studied her face. "What did you find out?" he asked.

"Cecil's going to surgery. I've got to call his family."

J.T. stood close by while she made the calls.

"They're on their way," she said a little while later. "They're all taking the first plane out of Kansas City to O'Hare."

"You really care about him, don't you?" J.T. asked.

"I do, but the problem is he doesn't care much about me. I apparently remind him too much of his ex-wife."

"Remember Sally's the only woman he's ever been with, and she gave him a raw deal. He's a little leery. Give him time."

Eddie nodded, and looked down the hall toward surgery. "I hope I have that time," she said.

"Go find his doctor and tell them who he is. Find out how he's doing," J.T. said.

Eddie hesitated, turning to look at him. "Don't leave me here alone, please," she asked.

A pained look came over J.T.'s face. "Cecil's family will be here soon. I've got to go and find my wife."

Eddie nodded and embraced him.

"Now, go on and make sure they're taking good care of your man." He gave Eddie a little push down the hall. She gave him a last look goodbye before she squared her shoulders and went through the swinging doors toward surgery.

* * *

J.T. watched Eddie push through the doors. What a mess, he thought. Cecil shot, Teddi putting her own life in danger, and the law breathing on his heels. Teddi was one of two people whose life he'd give his own to save without hesitation. He had to get to her before it was too late. He quickened his step.

"You've reached the end of your road," a familiar voice said. J.T. caught his breath and turned slowly, staring into a pair of bright blue eyes he knew too well.

There was no point in running. Gerard would never have confronted him if every bolthole wasn't closed and twelve unseen guns pointed at him. "Shall we go?" Gerard asked. J.T. nodded and walked toward the exit, while Gerard closely followed.

Time never passed more slowly than when you waited, Eddie thought, draining what must have been her fifth cup of stale vending machine coffee The surgical waiting room walls were puke green. Appropriate, she thought. When would somebody come out and tell her anything? She wanted to break down that door and scream.

Teddi was going to have a fit that she didn't make J.T. stay with her. Well, Teddi was going to have to realize that making J.T. do anything he didn't want to do was beyond her. J.T. was a man and he was going to take care of his family the way he saw fit, no matter what. That was something that Teddi was going to have to deal with.

The swinging doors of the surgical suite opened, and Cecil's surgeon emerged. Eddie stood up, feeling frightened.

"He's going to be okay," she said.

Eddie whooped and hugged the surgeon with glee.
"When can I see him?" she asked.

"Soon, we'll let you in soon. The rest of his family is
coming?" he asked.

"Yes, they'll be here shortly."

The surgeon left and Eddie sank back in the chair
with the cup of cold coffee cradled in her hands and a
smile on her face. Soon, the doctor had said. The time
was already passing more quickly.

Teddi sat in a small room, her hands tied behind her
and a bright light shining in her face. The man held
up the floppy disk she'd copied the information on.
"What is the meaning of this?" he asked.

Teddi sat stony-faced, staring at a spot in the distance.

"No matter," he said. "We'll soon find out."

He handed the floppy to another man, who left the
room with it. "Can I get you something? A cup of coffee
maybe? You've had a long night, Mrs. Henderson."

He knew who she was. Teddi drew in a breath and
watched the first fingers of dawn creep through a window.

The man leaned close to Teddi and whispered in her
ear. "You realize you're going to have to tell us where
your husband is," the man said.

He straightened. "A shame really, he was such a good
worker bee."

The wisp that was left of Teddi's nerves snapped and
she spit at the man, her eyes burning. He calmly wiped
the spittle from his cheek.

"It's an even greater shame that he got you involved
in this," he said, as he straightened his cuff. "Well, I
suppose you can look at it like this. At long last, you'll
be together."

The man exited the room, leaving Teddi alone with thoughts of despair.

The taxi driver opened the laptop computer Teddi had left with him. He pushed the button she said would turn it on and jumped a little when the thing whirred and beeped. He plugged it into the phone like she said. So much power in such a tiny package. What would they think of next?

He scratched his head as he tried to remember the detailed instructions she left him. When he moved his finger on the little screen, an arrow on the computer moved with it. Clever. And so complicated.

He started to tap on the keys. He prayed he would get it all right. The woman said lives depended on him, maybe even her life. Now, that would be a terrible thing for such a fine young woman to lose her life. Her husband was a mighty lucky man.

Twenty-three

Darkness cannot drive out darkness; only light can do that. Hate cannot drive out hate; only love can do that.

—*Martin Luther King, Jr.*

Gerard signaled the other man to sit in the front of the limousine with the driver. "Get in," he said to J.T.

J.T. only hesitated a second before he got into the car. Gerard sat across from him. "Boy, I wouldn't try anything if I were you," he said, reading the tensing of J.T.'s muscles.

"I wouldn't dream of it, you taught me everything I know. Except you used to know better than to call me boy," J.T. said.

Gerard shrugged. "Things change," he said, leaning back in the leather seat of the limo.

"That they do," J.T. answered. "I used to think you were a man of honor."

"Everything's relative, and everybody does what they have to do, what they believe in." He poured himself a drink from the car's bar, offering some to J.T. with a gesture. J.T. didn't bother to respond.

"You know, I always liked you, J.T., and I had called off the dogs. But you should have stayed under like I told you, and things would have been fine. You got sloppy. Before, there was no way you'd let yourself be taken."

J.T. shrugged and looked out the window.

"Family makes a man soft," Gerard said. "That's one mistake that I never made. You should have minded your own business, son. Your family is going to suffer for your mistakes."

Now, Gerard had J.T.'s full attention. Gerard chuckled and leaned back in his seat. "Yes, family is a fighting man's weakness," he said.

"What game are you playing?" J.T. asked. "You knew two years ago that I didn't know anything, that Paul never gave me any concrete information."

"Things change," Gerard said. "Like I said, things change."

Cecil looked so small in the hospital bed hooked up to tubes and monitors. Eddie sat next to him and held his hand. "The doctor said you're doing fine," she said.

Cecil's eyes fluttered open, and he gave her a crooked smile. "That's good, because I feel like crap," he said.

"I called your family hours ago, they should be here any minute."

Cecil squeezed her hand. "I'm glad you're here, Eddie. Thanks for sticking around."

She kissed him softly on the cheek. "It's the least I could do."

A nurse came bustling in and gave a pointed glance at Eddie. "I'd better step out now. I'll be back."

Eddie returned to the waiting room with a smile on her face. Cecil was going to be all right.

A tall, honey-skinned woman stormed into the waiting room. Eddie looked up in surprise.

"I find out from Cecil's brother that my baby's been shot and he's in the hospital," the woman yelled. "And here you are, that ol' lowdown tramp Eddie standing in for her sister as usual. How dare you two run off with my man!"

Eddie stood up slowly. "Sally Jennings, you're obviously drunk in addition to being out of your mind. You'd best get your finger out of my face," Eddie said.

The other family in the waiting room watched the confrontation with fascination.

Sally dropped her purse to the ground. "Why, you *slut,*" she spat. Sally threw the first punch and then the fight was on.

Hours had passed and the sun grew higher in the sky. Teddi had prayed until she had nothing left. She must have failed. If the taxi driver followed her instructions, it should have been all over by now.

Every muscle in her body ached from hours of sitting in that hard chair, with her hands tied behind her back. Her weariness was bone-deep. The waiting was so hard, she almost wished they'd come back in. Get it over with. She closed her eyes and a picture of Sylvie laughing flashed before her, then the feel of J.T.'s tender kisses. She'd had a good life, the best, filled with blessings. No woman could ask for more. Except to see my daughter grow up.

Tears leaked down her cheeks, and she shook her head. When that man came back in, she wanted to hold her head high. She didn't want to go out crying. She wanted to look that man proudly in the eye when he came back in, and hold him accountable for what he did.

* * *

The taxi driver opened the program like Teddi had instructed him. Ah, there it was, she'd managed to send the file to him. A grin spread over his face. That little lady was something.

He dug in one pocket, then another for the piece of paper she'd given him with the what had she called it? E-mail addresses, that was it. With triumph he finally pulled the paper out of his back pants pocket and smoothed it out. There were more than twenty E-mail addresses listed on the paper. The White House, CNN, the *Washington Post, New York Times,* all the networks, and more. There was a message he was to send with the file, also.

He'd better get to work. There was a lot to do. He bent over the computer and laboriously started pecking out the message. This computer stuff wasn't bad he thought. Much safer than driving a taxi. Maybe he wasn't too old to make a change after all.

Eddie sat on the hard bench in the jail cell. The woman sitting next to her stank, but she dare not draw away. One fight was enough for a day. She picked at the long reddish hairs that clung between her fingers and on her clothes, the result of the copious amount of Sally's weave she'd pulled out. She guessed they put Sally in a different cell.

The woman was berserk. Eddie had never had the experience of physically fighting for her life, but this had come close. They'd demolished the waiting room. The police had been called, and this was the result.

The cell bars clanged open. "Thompson," the warden called. Eddie got up and followed the woman.

Cecil's mother stood waiting for her. "I met your bail. I'm so sorry, Eddie," she said.

"What was the call for that woman attacking me?" 'Eddie asked. "What's wrong with that woman?"

"Unfortunately, quite a bit. She made Cecil's life a living hell, but he always stuck by her, until recently." She smiled at Eddie. "He's asking for you," she said. "You seem to have made quite an impression on him."

Eddie smiled. Then, with a worried look, she looked over her shoulder and asked, "Did you bail out Sally, too?"

Mrs. Jennings looked troubled. "The police couldn't calm her down. She's in a locked ward at the hospital."

"Geez," Eddie said.

"Sally has had a very hard life. Her father was . . . abusive, and she can't seem to quite get over it," Mrs. Jennings said. "She has major problems waiting for her back in Kansas. She's probably going to be in custody for a while."

"What happened?"

"They found out that she was the one who sent the fake bomb, and then blew up your sister's garage. She imagined Teddi and Cecil were having an affair, and that's why he wouldn't reconcile with her."

Eddie was speechless. "So, it was Sally all the time," she finally said.

Mrs. Jennings nodded. "She's one sick puppy," she said.

A phone rang in the limo. Gerard sighed and reached into his jacket, pulling out a cellular phone. "You got the disk, right? So why are you calling me? You know what to do, get rid of her."

Gerard pulled down the antenna and smiled benignly at J.T. "That was about your wife. She was picked up early this morning after breaking into the NIA offices."

One quick movement, as lightning fast as a snake, J.T. was holding the jagged glass edges of a broken bottle between Gerard's legs. "You make one sound, one wrong movement, and you're going to be singing soprano for the rest of your life," he said in a conversational tone.

Gerard paled. "Now, carefully and very slowly, ease that phone out of your pocket. You know what I want you to do. I want Teddi on a plane to Kansas in 15 minutes."

Gerard's muscles tensed. "Don't even think about it, boy," J.T. said. "You know right about now, I'd love to turn your family jewels into rocky mountain oysters. And I got more reason to do it than general principles."

Gerard eased the phone out and flipped it open. "There's a change of plan. Let the woman go and put her on a plane back to Kansas." He paused. "We can still use her."

"You'll never get out of this alive," Gerard said.

"The chance you'll get out of this intact is dropping with each passing minute. You were careless, Gerard."

"Not that careless. I always leave the microphone on. Look and see."

J.T. slowly looked up and saw the barrel of a gun trained on him through the separating glass of the limo.

The cellular phone rang again. "Maybe that's about your wife. I'm happily going to rescind the order I just made," Gerard said. He listened intently for a minute, and jerkily reached out and turned on the television.

"Breaking news is that high-level government officials are accused of conspiring against the present administration. Indictments have been issued . . ."

Gerard turned off the television and leaned back in his seat, trembling. "It's all over," he said.

And J.T. started to laugh.

Twenty-four

Delight thyself also in the LORD; and he shall give
thee the desires of thine heart.
—*Psalms, 37:4, the Holy Bible, King James Version*

"Pull over," Gerard ordered. The driver pulled over
to the shoulder of the highway.

Gerald looked at J.T. a long moment. "Your wife
is . . ." He shook his head. "She's something else. Go
back to your family, J.T."

J.T. stared at him in disbelief. "Go on, get out of
here," Gerard said, with a sigh, pushing a button. The
locks clicked, and J.T. scrambled out of the car. The
limo pulled off, leaving nothing but dust in its wake.

Eddie sat at Cecil's bedside. He was asleep, and she
took his hand in hers. What was it about the strong,
quiet man that drew her so?

She bit her lip and looked away. What if he didn't
want her here? He thought she was like his wife. Eddie
shuddered. She was nothing like that woman.

"Eddie," Cecil said. Startled at his voice, she flinched.

He squeezed her hand. "I'm happy to see you here," he said. His voice was dry and strained. Eddie poured ice water into his cup and held it to his lips.

"I don't want to leave. I realize that you think I'm like your wife, but I've grown to . . . to care for you," she said, as she carefully sat the cup back down.

"You're nothing like Sally. She would never stay here beside me for hours in this dingy hospital. I care about you, Eddie, and I need you here with me."

He reached for her, and she laid her face against his shoulder, and the silence between them held the beginning of a promise.

Teddi felt like a sponge someone had wrung out and set out to dry. When the man came back, she'd been ready, she'd been strong. He'd untied her hands and told her to follow him. He'd led her to the roof where she supposed he would shoot her. Instead, a helicopter waited. They landed at Kennedy airport, where another man met her and put her on a plane to Kansas City. First class, no less.

She was too weary to hope, too tired to pray anymore. She joined the stream of passengers that spilled into the airport concourse.

"Teddi," she heard a familiar and much loved voice call. She looked around and there he was, J.T. and Sylvie, waving wildly.

Teddi choked and stumbled toward her family and the next thing she knew, she was wrapped in her husband's strong arms. She clung to him and Sylvie, sobbing while J.T. rocked them, cradled in his arms.

"Here we are in Dixon, Kansas, the home of the courageous Hendersons who singlehandedly brought the

NIA conspirators to justice," the news anchor spoke into the camera. "Here comes Justine Thompson, Teddi Henderson's mother, right now. Do you have anything you'd like to say, Mrs. Thompson?"

"Why don't you get that microphone out of my face and help me carry these groceries in like a gentleman?"

Teddi laughed a deep, rich contralto laugh. "Mama sure did set that reporter straight," she said to J.T. "The media should know better than to descend on Dixon, Kansas, en masse."

They all sat in the den in front of the TV, Teddi and J.T. on the couch, Sylvie at their feet. Teddi had just awakened from a well-deserved nap.

The doorbell rang. "Are they here already?" J.T. asked.

"It's the last day of Kwanzaa, and I'm hungry, c'mon."

J.T. dropped a playful kiss on the tip of her nose. "This is the first time on the seventh day of Kwanzaa I haven't seen you glued to the stove all day."

"I had more exciting things to do, Mr. Henderson," Teddi murmured.

The doorbell rang again and Sylvie skipped toward the front door. "I'm going to let them in, I'm hungry."

The house filled with people, family, neighbors, and friends, all bearing bowls and dishes, and full of congratulations, well-wishes, and good food.

Teddi's father beamed when he hugged his daughter. "I'm so proud of you," he said. "You put your family first and God took care of the rest.

"He always does, Dad," she said.

John watched Justine busily setting out the dishes. "There's nothing in life more important than the ones you love," he said. "Sometimes you don't realize your blessings until you lose them."

J.T. approached with his catlike walk and overheard

John's words. He wrapped his arms around Teddi's waist, pulling her back against him. "My blessings are in this room, and in my arms," he said. "Mr. Peel at the utility company wants to hire me to work with their computer systems."

Teddi whooped with joy. "You knew I didn't want to leave, didn't you?" she said.

He touched her nose. "I knew Dixon is the place for us. I want to work on expanding our family like you'd mentioned some years ago, and there's no better place that I'd care to raise our children."

A slow smile grew on Teddi's face. She thought she once knew what contentment was years ago. But her father was right, you don't savor true happiness until you learned loss and experienced the redemption of having every blessing restored.

They feasted on ham and turkey and sweet potato pie. Yams and black-eyed peas and hoppin' john were set out along with steaming bowls of collard greens and chitlins. Cornbread and rolls, yellow pound cake, and fresh-baked cherry pies rounded out the spread.

"This is as good as the Karamu was," Sylvie said. "Mrs. Peel said she's going to see if she can get some African drummers from Kansas City for next year's Karamu."

Teddi grinned, it seemed that Kwanzaa was here to stay in Dixon, Kansas. Her home was filled with her family and every sort of people, of every color and background, all celebrating the seventh day of Kwanzaa. And that's the way it should be, Teddi thought with satisfaction.

"Teddi, your sister wants to talk to you," J.T. said, holding out the phone.

"Listen up, everybody," Teddi said after she hung up

he phone. "Eddie says Cecil is doing fine, and he'll be oming home next week."

A relieved murmur grew in the room.

"She's staying in Chicago with him until he comes ack," she whispered to J.T. "It looks as if Cecil's the nan to settle Eddie down."

After everyone had eaten their fill, Sylvie lit all seven f the candles. Red, green, and black, they glowed with he fire of life, love, and family, with the renewal of alues and principles held dear.

"Habari gani?" Teddi asked. What is the news? The news was Imani fulfilled. The story they'd tell tonight vas their own. Their family was together, bonded with ove, and a part of a closely knit community that cared bout each other. The circle had closed, and Teddi's heart was complete. Full circle. The end of the story vas only the beginning, and the cycle of love and family vould continue forever.

Author's Note

The Kwanzaa celebration revolves around common principles, traditions, and rituals. The holiday is one of the heart, springing from values and principles rather than any ritual or practice. The way Teddi and her family celebrate Kwanzaa is only one of many ways. Look at the rituals and recipes as a guide, not an absolute, and if any of you feel called to celebrate Kwanzaa, let it come from your heart, and make it your own.

Kwanzaa, like so many of our holidays, revolves around the food; food prepared with care and shared with loved ones. Teddi's meals are such an integral part of her, I felt called to include recipes to this story. Simple food, with easy to find ingredients, like I like to prepare, and my family likes to eat.

This was more of a challenge than I expected. Like the main character, I'm a dash here, a splash there, a sprinkle of this, and a touch of that type of cook. The very definition of a recipe includes measurements. So, occasionally, I left out some spices and herbs I add to the dishes merely because figuring out the exact measurements was beyond me.

So, please, try the recipes at your own risk, and like the holiday of Kwanzaa, make them your own. Add spices and herbs to your own taste, a touch of ginger here, thyme here, parsley and maybe a bay leaf or two.

The Recipes

Grandma Louise's Kansas Fried Chicken	219
String Beans and New Potatoes	219
Teddi's Biscuits	220
Jollof Rice	221
West African Collard Greens and Cabbage	222
Yam Balls	222
West African Chin-Chin Cookies	223
Ginger Beer	223
J.T.'s Favorite Pork Chops	225
Sylvie's Yum Cheese and Macaroni	226
Meat Patties	227
Pork and Chicken Jerk	228
Jamaican Rice and Peas	229
Pineapple Fool	229
Injera (Ethiopian Bread)	231
Doro Wat	232
Egyptian Brown Fava Beans	232
Axum Salad	233
Honey Wine	233
Brazilian Barbecue and Sauce	235
Farova de Ovo	236
Brazilian Rice	237
Dakar Fish	239

Akara Balls   240
West African Coconut Pie   240
Black-Eyed Peas for Luck   241
Cornbread   241
Collard Greens for Foldin' Money   242
Baked Glazed Ham   242
Sweet Potato Pie   243
Chitlins   243
Pecan Yams   244
Yellow Pound Cake   244

J.T.'s First Meal Back at Home

Grandma Louise's Kansas Fried Chicken

- 1 chicken, cut into pieces
   Lemon juice from 4–5 lemons
- 1½ cups flour
- 1 tsp. salt
- 1 tsp. black pepper
- 2 cups vegetable oil

Put chicken in a bowl and sprinkle with lemon juice, allow to marinate at least 2 hours. Combine salt, pepper, and flour in a large plastic bag. Drop each marinated chicken piece into flour and shake until coated. Heat oil in a cast iron skillet until a pinch of flour sizzles. Cook chicken a batch at a time until golden brown (around 30 minutes). Drain on paper towels and serve.

String Beans and New Potatoes

- ½ lb. bacon ends or bits and pieces
- 2 lb. fresh green beans, snapped

    1 lb. new potatoes, scraped
    2 onions, diced
       Sprinkle of cayenne pepper
       Salt and pepper

Fry bacon until barely crisp, drain grease. Add green beans, onion, salt, and cayenne. Cover with water and boil around 20 minutes. Then add new potatoes, boil until potatoes are soft. Season with salt and pepper to taste.

Teddi's Biscuits

    2 cups flour
    ½ cup Crisco
    1 tbsp. baking powder
    1 tsp. salt
    ¼ cup milk

Preheat oven to 425 degrees. Mix together dry ingredients and cut in Crisco to coarse crumbs. Add milk and mix until dough is just moist. Knead on floured surface a few times. Don't over-knead. Roll out dough until about ½ inch thick and cut with 2-inch cutter or glass. Bake for 12 to 15 minutes until barely golden.

The First Day of Kwanzaa

Food from the Land of Our Ancestors: West Africa

Jollof Rice

2 lb. chicken, cut into 1-inch pieces
½ cup vegetable oil
¾ cup yellow onions, chopped
1 15-oz. can tomatoes, diced
2 6-oz. cans tomato paste
1 qt. water
1 tbsp. salt
½ tsp. black pepper
1 tsp. crushed red pepper
2 cups white rice

Saute chicken and onion in vegetable oil until browned. Remove chicken and add rice to oil, and cook until hot. Add diced tomatoes, tomato paste, salt, peppers, and water. Cover and simmer on low. Stir in chicken when rice is soft and liquid is absorbed.

West African Collard Greens and Cabbage

          2 lb. cabbage
          2 lb. collard greens
        ½ lb. bacon
          1 large yellow onion, chopped
          1 tbsp. salt
          1 tsp. black pepper
          1 qt. water
          1 oz. butter

Simmer collards, bacon, onion, salt, and peppers in water for half an hour. Add cabbage and butter and cook for 15 minutes more.

Yam Balls

          3 lb. yams
          3 eggs
        ½ cup evaporated milk
          2 tbsp. onions, finely chopped
        ¼ tsp. garlic powder
          1 tsp. salt
          4 tbsp. flour

Add salt to water and boil yams until soft. Drain, and after they're cool, peel and mash them. Add the other ingredients, mix thoroughly, and chill for an hour. Form into 2-inch balls and deep fat fry at 360 degrees until golden brown.

West African Chin-Chin cookies

- 4 eggs
- ½ cup sugar
- 2 cups self-rising flour
- 2 tsp. cinnamon
- 1 tbsp. orange rind, grated
- 4 oz. (½ cup) butter

Beat eggs and add sugar, set aside. Add cinnamon and orange rind to flour and cut in butter like you do for pie crust. Blend in egg mixture. Knead until smooth, roll the dough out on a floured board, and cut into shapes. Then deep fat fry the cookies at 375 degrees until golden brown.

Ginger Beer

- 2 gal. water
- 1 lb. fresh ginger, chopped fine
- 1 cup honey
- 2 tsp. yeast
- 3½ cups molasses

Add water to ginger and honey in a large pot, heat to boiling, then cool to lukewarm. Add yeast dissolved in ½ cup lukewarm water. Cover and allow to stand overnight in a warm place. The next day add molasses, chill, and strain. Refrigerate.

The Second Day of Kwanzaa:

Foods from Lands of the
Diaspora: North America

J.T.'s Favorite Pork Chops

 1 cup flour
 1 tsp. seasoned salt
 1/2 tsp. pepper
 1/8 tsp. cayenne pepper
 2 tbsp. vegetable oil
 1 tsp. sugar
 1 tsp. cinnamon
 1 tsp. lemon juice
    Vegetable oil for frying
 4 apples, cored and unpeeled, thinly sliced in rounds
10 center-cut pork chops, split to the bone

Mix together flour, salt, and peppers, and set aside. Mix sugar, oil, lemon juice, and cinnamon. Marinate chops and apples in the mixture at least 30 minutes or more. Arrange slices in splits of pork chops. Coat chops with seasoned flour. Fry over moderate heat until browned, and then place in an ovenproof dish and bake 35 minutes at 350 degrees.

Sylvie's Yum Cheese and Macaroni

½ lb. elbow macaroni
½ stick (4 tbsp.) butter
1 12-oz. can evaporated milk
1 lb. grated cheese (Sylvie likes medium cheddar)
2 eggs, beaten
 Salt and pepper to taste

Preheat oven to 350 degrees. Boil macaroni in salted water until barely done. Drain and toss with butter in large ovenproof bowl. Stir about ⅔ cup of the milk into the macaroni, then add eggs and ¾ of the cheese. Season to taste with salt and pepper, and set dish in oven. Every 5 minutes or so, remove bowl briefly, stirring in some of the reserved cheese and milk to keep mixture moist and smooth. After all the cheese and milk has been mixed in and the mixture is creamy, bake it around 20 more minutes until heated through.

Teddi served these dishes with baked sweet potatoes slathered in real butter, sweet peas, homemade rolls, and a tossed green salad. She didn't bother with dessert. She knew nobody'd have room.

The Third Day of Kwanzaa:

Foods from Lands of the Diaspora: Jamaica

(Slightly adapted for Kansas ingredients and taste)

Meat Patties

½ lb. ground beef
½ lb. ground pork
1 tsp. powdered red pepper
½ cup onion, chopped
½ cup green onions (scallions), chopped
¼ cup celery, chopped
¼ cup red bell pepper, chopped
2 cloves garlic, minced
1 tsp. seasoned salt
1 tsp. dried thyme
2 tsp. soy sauce
½ cup bread crumbs
1 tbsp. all-purpose flour
2 cans large refrigerator biscuits
1 egg yolk, beaten with 1 tbsp. milk

Preheat oven to 375 degrees. Brown ground meat, drain off excess fat. Add spices, soy sauce and chopped vegetables. Cook until celery and onion are translucent. Stir in bread crumbs and flour, mix well. Then on floured board, roll out biscuits to 6-inch circles and place about 3 tbsp. of meat in the center. Fold biscuit dough over to make crescents, and crimp edges with a fork. Brush crusts with beaten egg in milk. Bake at 375 for ½ hour or until golden brown.

Pork and Chicken Jerk

4 tbsp. ground allspice
2 onions, finely chopped
2 jalapeno peppers, seeded and finely chopped
3 cloves garlic, finely chopped
1 tsp. ground cinnamon
1 tsp. ground nutmeg
6 bay leaves, crumbled
1 tsp. salt
1 tsp. pepper
3 tbsp. vinegar
1 cup vegetable oil
2 lb. lean pork, cut into ½ inch chunks
1 chicken, cut into ½ inch chunks

Mix all ingredients except the meat together into a paste. Rub meat with mixture, then cover meat and allow to marinate at least 2 hours. Grill for around 2 hours or roast in oven for an hour. Serve with raw onions.

Jamaican Rice and Peas

2 15-oz. cans small red beans (when she lived in New York, Teddi used 3 cups cooked pidgeon peas)
4 cups coconut milk
½ cup green onions, chopped
½ teaspoon ground thyme
1 cup white rice
1½ cups water

Mix ingredients together in large pot and bring to a boil. Then reduce heat to simmer and cook for about 25 minutes or until all the water is absorbed and rice is fluffy.

Pineapple Fool

2 cups pineapple, finely chopped
1¼ cups heavy cream
1½ tsp. vanilla extract
3 tbsp. powdered sugar

Drain pineapple well in a colander. Whip cream with vanilla and 1 tbsp. powdered sugar until peaks form. Chill fruit and cream separately for an hour. Just before serving, fold cream into fruit and sprinkle with remaining powdered sugar.

The Fourth Day of Kwanzaa:

Food from Our Ancient Roots

Injera (Ethiopian Bread)

A thin fermented soft bread made from teff, a grain indigenous to Ethiopia. Here's an adapted version.

4 cups self-rising flour
1 cup whole-wheat flour
1 tsp. baking powder
2 cups club soda
4 cups water
   Vegetable oil

Add water and club soda to flours and baking powder in large bowl. Beat to smooth, thin batter. Heat 2 tbsp. vegetable oil, spread ½ cup of batter thinly. Remove from heat and swirl batter until it makes a very thin pancake. Don't brown or crisp.

Stack on large platter lined with a clean cotton dish towel. Line serving platter with the bread, and fold into quarters to pinch off pieces with the right hand and use it to scoop up the food.

Doro Wat

1 chicken, chopped into ½-inch pieces, with bones
¼ cup lemon juice
Water
3 cups Bermuda onions, finely chopped
3 oz. butter
½ tsp. cayenne pepper
1 tsp. paprika (to give the dish its characteristic color)
½ tsp. black pepper
¼ tsp. ginger
8 eggs, hard-boiled

Soak chicken in 2 cups water to which the lemon juice has been added. Brown Bermuda onions, without fat added, until very dark, stirring constantly. Add butter and seasonings and 1 cup water. Blend together and simmer on low, while draining water from chicken. Then add chicken, and simmer until chicken is tender. Add water if necessary to maintain a stew texture. Before serving, peel eggs and add them to the Doro Wat.

Egyptian Brown Fava Beans
(Teddi ordered them a while back)

3 tbsp. olive oil
2 cups cooked brown fava beans
3 cloves garlic, minced
Salt and pepper
2-4 eggs, hard-boiled
½ cup fresh parsley, chopped
Lemon wedges

Heat oil in saucepan, add beans, garlic, salt, and pepper to taste, mix, and cook until heated through. Place hard-boiled eggs in bowl, cover with beans, sprinkle with parsley. Place lemon wedges on the side.

Axum Salad

1½ lb. firm tomatoes, chopped
½ cup sweet onions, chopped
1 clove garlic, minced
1 hot chili pepper (optional), finely chopped

Marinate in sauce of:

1 cup ketchup
¼ cup vinegar
½ cup oil
½ cup sweet white wine
1 tsp. Worcestershire sauce
1 tsp. salt
¼ tsp. black pepper
A few drops Tabasco sauce

Then drain well, serve and eat with injera bread.

Honey Wine

1 pint mild-flavored medium-dry white wine
1 pt. water
4 tbsp. honey

Blend together and chill until very cold. Serve with fresh fruit for dessert. Teddi sprinkles a few chopped dates over a simple fruit salad of oranges, grapes, and bananas.

The Fifth Day of Kwanzaa:

Food from Lands of the Diaspora: Brazil

Brazilian Barbecue and Sauce

$\frac{1}{2}$ lb. link pork sausage
1 chicken, cut into pieces
$\frac{1}{2}$ lb. $\frac{1}{2}$-inch-thick pork loin steaks
$\frac{1}{2}$ lb. $\frac{1}{2}$-inch-thick boneless beef steaks
9 cloves garlic, minced
1 tbsp. red pepper flakes
1 tsp. paprika
2 cups water
   Salt and pepper

Soak meat in water mixed with seasonings for at least an hour. Then grill. Make sure the pork is well done.

Cold Brazilian Barbecue Sauce

1 onion, finely chopped
1 green pepper, finely chopped
2 fresh tomatoes, peeled and chopped
2 green onions, chopped
½ cup fresh parsley, chopped
½ cup vinegar
3 tbsp. olive oil
   Salt and pepper

Mix together and refrigerate an hour or so before serving.

Farova de Ovo
(Teddi substitutes bread crumbs for the manoic flour, which she can find nowhere in Dixon, Kansas.)

6 tbsp. butter
2 onions, finely chopped
12 black olives, pitted
½ cup cooked ham, diced
4 eggs, lightly beaten
1 cup unseasoned bread crumbs
   Salt and pepper
   Chopped fresh parsley for garnish

Melt butter in skillet, add onions, olives, and ham and cook over medium heat until onions are translucent. Then add eggs and cook until soft scrambled. Add bread crumbs, mix well, salt and pepper to taste.

Brazilian Rice

2 tbsp. vegetable oil
1 onion, thinly sliced
1 green bell pepper, finely chopped and seeded
3 cloves garlic, minced
1 cup white rice, uncooked
2 fresh tomatoes, peeled and finely chopped
$\frac{1}{2}$ tsp. salt

Cook onion, green pepper, and garlic in oil in large skillet. Cook until soft and add rice, coat with oil and cook until hot (about 2 minutes). Add water and salt, bring to a boil, reduce heat to simmer, cover, and cook for about another 20 minutes until rice is done. Remove from heat and add tomatoes before serving.

Served with a tossed green salad and fresh tropical fruits for dessert.

The Sixth Day of Kwanzaa:

West African Dishes Teddi planned to bring to the Dixon, Kansas, Karamu Potluck Celebration

Dakar Fish

1 onion, finely chopped
½ cup green peppers, finely chopped
½ cup vegetable oil
1 tsp. salt
½ tsp. cayenne pepper
1 stick (½) cup butter
1 6-oz. can tomato paste
2 cups water
4 lb. fish fillets
1 large cabbage, cut into 8 wedges
4 sweet potatoes, peeled and halved

Cook onions and green pepper in vegetable oil until translucent in a Dutch oven. Add salt and cayenne pepper and tomato paste. Blend mixture with water until smooth. Lay fish at bottom of pan, and lay cabbage and sweet potatoes on top. Cover tightly and simmer on low for about an hour until vegetables are done.

Akara Balls

1 lb. black-eyed peas
½ tsp. cayenne pepper
1 tsp. salt
½ cup onion, finely chopped
   Enough vegetable oil for deep frying

Soak beans overnight, until soft. Run through blender or food processor with seasoning and onions with enough water to achieve a thick batter consistency. Drop by teaspoonful into hot oil and fry until golden brown.

West African Coconut Pie

2 pie crusts for 9-inch pie pan (Teddi uses packaged pie crust, but you can make your own.)
6 oz. (1½ sticks) butter
½ cup sugar
2 eggs, beaten
2 cups moist grated coconut
1 cup milk
1 tsp. vanilla
¼ tsp. baking soda

Line pie pan with crust and bake until lightly browned. Cream butter and sugar together, add eggs, then coconut, milk, vanilla, and baking soda. Pour into pie crust. Cut second crust into strips and cross-hatch them on top of pie. Flute edges and bake at 350 degrees for 40 minutes or until golden brown.

The Seventh Day of Kwanzaa:

Traditional African-American New Year's Day Dishes

Black-Eyed Peas for Luck

1 lb. black-eyed peas, cleaned and soaked
6 cups water
½ lb. smoked ham hocks
1 onion, chopped
1 tsp. salt
¼ tsp. cayenne pepper

Put everything in a Dutch oven and simmer on low for a couple of hours.

Cornbread

2¼ cups plain flour
1½ cups yellow cornmeal
10 tsp. baking powder
½ tsp. salt

      2 cups milk
      2 eggs
      2 tbsp. butter
    1/4 cup sugar, if desired

Mix dry ingredients together in large bowl. Beat milk
and eggs together and add. Melt butter and stir it in.
Pour into a greased pan and bake at 375 degrees for
about 30 minutes or until golden brown.

Collard Greens for Foldin' Money

      2 lb. collard greens
      1 lb. pork neckbones
         Sprinkle of cayenne pepper
      1 tsp. vinegar
         Salt and pepper to taste

Simmer neckbones until they're falling off the bone in
a large pot. Remove neckbones with a slotted spoon,
take meat off bones, dice it, and return meat to pot.
Add greens, vinegar, and cayenne pepper to neckbone
broth and cook on low heat until greens are tender.
Salt and pepper to taste.

Baked Glazed Ham

12- to 15- lb. ham (not the shank end)
        1 qt. real maple syrup
        2 tbsp. dry mustard
           Whole cloves

Trim ham but leave some fat. Score fat 1/4 inch down
to meat in a diamond pattern. Then take an ice pick
and stab ham multiple times all over. Take dry mustard
and massage into ham, then stick whole cloves into

icepick holes, evenly spaced. Put ham into a deep roasting dish and pour maple syrup over it. Put ham in a cold oven and cook at 300 degrees for 30 minutes, then reduce heat to 250 and turn ham over. Cook 3 hours for 12-lb. ham, and add 30 minutes for each 2 lb. over that. Turn ham every 30 minutes. When ham is done, drain on a rack and slice.

Sweet Potato Pie

   2 cups sweet potatoes, cooked and mashed
 $\frac{1}{4}$ cup butter
   3 eggs
   1 cup milk
 $1\frac{1}{4}$ cup sugar
 $\frac{1}{4}$ tsp. salt
 $\frac{1}{4}$ tsp. nutmeg
   1 tsp. vanilla
 $\frac{1}{4}$ cup orange juice
   1 9-inch pie shell, unbaked

Mix all ingredients and pour into pie shell. Bake at 425 degrees for 15 minutes, then lower heat to 350 degrees and bake for an additional $1\frac{1}{2}$ hours or until done.

Chitlins

  10 lb. chitterlings, cleaned very well
   1 cup vinegar
   1 tbsp. sugar
   2 tbsp. seasoned salt
   1 onion, diced
   4 fresh hot red peppers, diced

To clean chitterlings, soak them in warm salt water at least an hour. Cut each into 6-inch pieces and split them, removing all fat and any visible debris. Then wash in hot water 5 to 10 times. The secret is to clean them very well. Teddi won't eat just anybody's chitlins. Place all ingredients in a large pot, and simmer on low at least 4 hours.

(Grandma Louise says a peeled Irish potato in the pot will keep the smell down while the chitlins are cooking.)

Pecan Yams

> 3 cups sweet potatoes, mashed
> 2 eggs, beaten
> ¼ cup milk
> 1 cup sugar
> 1 tsp. vanilla
> ½ cup (4 oz.) butter

Mix ingredients and place in a baking dish, then combine:

> 1 cup brown sugar
> ⅓ cup flour
> 1 cup pecans, chopped
> ½ cup (4 oz.) butter, melted

Drizzle mixture over yams in the baking dish and bake at 350 degrees for 30 minutes.

Yellow Pound Cake

> 2 cups all-purpose flour
> 1¼ cups sugar
> 1 tsp. salt
> 1 tsp. baking powder
> ¾ cup butter
> ½ cup milk

> 1 tsp. vanilla
> 3 eggs

Preheat oven to 300 degrees. Sift flour, salt, and baking powder together. Cream butter and sugar together, add milk and vanilla. Add flour mixture slowly to the liquid, beating with electric mixer at low speed. Add eggs and beat at low speed for at least 3 minutes. Pour batter into a greased 9-inch loaf pan. Bake for 1½ hours or until knife or toothpick in center comes out clean. Cool completely before removing from loaf pan.

Books about Kwanzaa

Imani by Bridget Anderson in the *Moonlight and Mistletoe* anthology. Pinnacle Books (Arabesque) 1997

Kwanzaa: A Celebration of Family, Community and Culture by M. Karenga. University of Sankore Press, 1997. (Commemorative Edition.)

Kwanzaa: An African-American Celebration of Culture and Cooking by Eric Copage. William Morris & Company, 1993.

The Complete Kwanzaa: Celebrating Our Cultural Harvest by Dorothy Winbush Riley. HarperCollins, 1996.

Affirmations for a Year-Round Kwanzaa by Gwynelle Dismulkes. Winston-Derek, 1994.

Kwanzaa and Me: A Teacher's Story by Vivian Gussin Paley. Harvard University Press, 1996 (Reprint.)

A Kwanzaa Celebration: Festive Recipes and Homemade Gifts from an African-American Kitchen by Angela Shelf Medearis. Penguin USA, 1995.

A Kwanzaa Fable by Eric Copage. William Morrow & Co., 1995.

Kwanzaa: Everything You Always Wanted to Know but Didn't Know Where to Ask by Cedric McClester. Gumbs and Thomas, 1996.

Children's Books about Kwanzaa

Ages 4 to 8

The Story of Kwanzaa by Donna L. Washington, illustrated by Stephen Taylor. HarperCollins, 1997.

The Gifts of Kwanzaa by Synthia Saint James. Albert Whitman & Co., 1997.

t's Kwanzaa Time! by Linda and Clay Goss, illustrated by Ashley Bryan. Putnam Publishing Group, 1995.

Kwanzaa Crafts: A Holiday Craft Book by Judith Hoffman Corwin. Franklin Watts, 1995.

Kwanzaa Celebration: A Pop-Up Book by Nancy Williams, illustrated by Robert Sabuda. Little Simon, 1995.

My First Kwanzaa Book by Deborah M. Newton Chocolate, illustrated by Cal Massey. Cartwheel Co., 1992.

Seven Candles for Kwanzaa by Andrea Davis Pinkney, illustrated by Brian Pinkney. Dial Books, 1993.

Imani's Gift at Kwanzaa by Denise Burden-Patman, illustrated by Floyd Cooper. Aladdin Books, 1993.

Crafts For Kwanzaa by Kathy Ross, illustrated by Sharon Lane Holm. Millbrook Press, 1994.

Habari Gani? What's the News?: A Kwanzaa Story by Sundaira Morninghouse, illustrated by Jody Kim. Open Hand, 1992.

Ages 9 to 12

Kwanzaa Karamu: Cooking and Crafts for a Kwanzaa Feast by April A. Brady, illustrated by Barbara Knutson. Carolrhoda Books, 1995.

Kwanzaa Fun by Linda Robertson, illustrated by Julia Pearson. Kingfisher Books, 1996.

Celebrating Kwanzaa by Diane Hoyt-Goldsmith, photography by Lawrence Migdale. Holiday House, 1994.

The Children's Book of Kwanzaa: A Guide to Celebrating the Holiday by Delores Johnson. Aladdin Paperbacks, 1997.

The Seven Days of Kwanzaa by Andrea Shelf Madearis. Scholastic Paperbacks, 1997.

A Very Special Kwanzaa by Deborah M. Newton Chocolate. Scholastic Paperbacks, 1996.

Kwanzaa: Why We Celebrate it the Way We Do by Martin and Kate Hintz. Capstone Press, 1996.

Books about Rosa Parks

Rosa Parks: My Story by Rosa Parks. Dial Books, 1992.
Quiet Strength: The Faith, the Hope and the Heart of a Woman Who Changed a Nation by Rosa Parks and Gregory J. Reed. Zondervan, 1995.

Children 9 to 12

Rosa Parks by Eloise Greenfield, illustrated by Gil Ashby. HarperCollins, 1996.
Rosa Parks: Fight for Freedom by Keith Brandt, illustrated by Gershom Griffith. Troll Associates, 1993.

Children 4 to 8

I Am Rosa Parks by Rosa Parks and James Haskins, illustrated by Wil Clay. Dial Books, 1997.

Books about Sojourner Truth

Sojourner Truth: A Life, a Symbol by Neil Irvin Painter. W. W. Norton & Co., 1997.
The Narrative of Sojourner Truth by Margaret Washington. Vintage Books, 1993.
Glorying in Tribulation: The Lifework of Sojourner Truth by Erlene Stetson and Linda David. Michigan State University Press, 1994.

Children 9 to 12

Sojourner Truth: Ain't I a Woman? by Patricia and Fred McKissack. Scholastic Paperbacks, 1994.

Books about Harriet Tubman

Harriet Tubman by Robert Hogrogian. January Productions, 1979.
Harriet Tubman: Slavery and the Underground Railroad by Megan McClard. Silver Burdett, 1991.

Children 9 to 12

Freedom Train by Dorothy Sterling. Scholastic Paperbacks, 1991.
Harriet Tubman: Conductor on the Underground Railroad by Ann Petry. HarperCollins, 1996.

Children 4 to 8

Aunt Harriet's Underground Railroad by Faith Ringgold. Crown, 1994.

Books about Madame C. J. Walker

Madame C. J. Walker by Cookie Lommel. Holloway Press, 1993.

Children 9 to 12

Doing It For Yourself: A Tammy and Owen Adventure with Madame C. J. Walker by Tonya Bolden, illustrated by Luther Knox. Corporation for Cultural Literacy, 1997.

Children 4 to 8

Madame C. J. Walker: Building a Business Empire by Penny Colman. Millbrook, 1994.

Books about Cinque of the *Amistad*

Amistad by David Pesci. Shooting Star, 1998.
Black Odyssey:The Case of the Slave Ship Amistad by Mary Cable. Penguin USA, 1998.
Mutiny on the Amistad by Howard Jones. Oxford University Press, 1997.
The Amistad Slave Revolt and American Abolition by Karen Zeinert. Linnet Books, 1997.

Children 9 to 12

Amistad Rising: A Story of Freedom by Veronica V. Chambers, Shelly Bowen, Allyn Johnston, illustrated by Paul Lee, Harcourt, Brace & Co., 1998

Books about Zora Neale Hurston

Dust Tracks on a Road by Zora Neale Hurston. Harper-Collins, 1998.
Jump at De Sun: The Story of Zora Neale Hurston by A. P. Porter. First Avenue Editions, 1992.
Sorrow's Kitchen: The Life and Folklore of Zora Neale Hurston by Mary E. Lyons. Atheneum, 1990.
Every Tub Must Sit on Its Own Bottom: The Philosophy and Politics of Zora Neale Hurston by Deborah G. Plant. University of Illinois Press, 1995.

Dear Readers:

Happy Kwanzaa! I hope this book was enlightening if you didn't know a lot about Kwanzaa, enriching if you did, and most of all, an entertaining read.

My follow-up to *Heart's Desire,* the story of Kara's best friend, Taylor, will be on the shelves July 1999. I promise mystery, suspense, and lots of love.

Write me with your thoughts at P.O. Box 654, Topeka, KS 66601, and include a SASE if you like. Have a wonderful, loving holiday season, and good reading!

Sincerely, Monica Jackson

COMING IN JANUARY . . .

BEYOND DESIRE, by Gwynne Forster   (0-7860-0607-2, $4.99/$6.50)
Amanda Ross is pregnant and single. Certainly not a role model for junior high school students, the board of education may deny her promotion to principal if they learn the truth. What she needs is a husband and music engineer Marcus Hickson agrees to it. His daughter needs surgery and Amanda will pay the huge medical bill. But love creeps in and soon theirs is an affair of the heart.

LOVE SO TRUE, by Loure Bussey   (0-7860-0608-0, $4.99/$6.50)
Janelle Sims defied her attraction to wealthy businessman Aaron Devereau because he reminded Janelle of her womanizing father. Yet he is the perfect person to back her new fashion boutique and she seeks him out. Now they are partners, friends . . . and lovers. But a cunning woman's lies separate them and Janelle must go to him to confirm their love.

ALL THAT GLITTERS, by Viveca Carlysle (0-7860-0609-9, $4.99/$6.50)
After her sister's death, Leigh Barrington inherited a huge share of Cassiopeia Salons, a chain of exclusive beauty parlors. The business was Leigh's idea in the first place and now she wants to run it her way. To retain control, Leigh marries board member Caesar Montgomery who is instantly smitten with her. When she may be the next target of her sister's killer, Leigh learns to trust in Caesar's love.

AT LONG LAST LOVE, by Bettye Griffin   (0-7860-0610-2, $4.99/$6.50)
Owner of restaurant chain Soul Food To Go, Kendall Lucas has finally found love with her new neighbor, Spencer Barnes. Until she discovers he owns the new restaurant that is threatening her business. They compromise, but Spencer learns Kendall has launched a secret advertising campaign. Embittered by her own lies, Kendall loses hope in their love. But she underestimates Spencer's devotion and his vow to make her his partner for life.

ROMANCES THAT SIZZLE
FROM ARABESQUE

FTER DARK, by Bette Ford (0-7860-0442-8, $4.99/$6.50)
aylor Hendricks' brother is the top NBA draft choice. She wants to protect
m from the lure of fame and wealth, but meets basketball superstar Donald
illiams in an exclusive Detroit restaurant. Donald is determined to prove
at she is wrong about him. In this game all is at stake . . . including Taylor's
eart.

EGUILED, by Eboni Snoe (0-7860-0046-5, $4.99/$6.50)
hen Raquel Mason agrees to impersonate a missing heiress for just one
ght and plans go awry, a daring abduction makes her the captive of seductive
ate Bowman. Together on a journey across exotic Caribbean seas to the
erilous wilds of Central America, desire looms in their hearts. But when the
asquerade is over, will their love end?

ONSPIRACY, by Margie Walker (0-7860-0385-5, $4.99/$6.50)
auline Sinclair and Marcellus Cavanaugh had the love of a lifetime. Until
auline had to leave everything behind. Now she's back and their love is as
rong as ever. But when the President of Marcellus's company turns up dead
d Pauline is the prime suspect, they must risk all to their love.

RE AND ICE, by Carla Fredd (0-7860-0190-9, $4.99/$6.50)
ears of being in the spotlight and a recent scandal regarding her ex-fianceé
d a supermodel, the daughter of a Georgia politician, Holly Aimes has turned
old. But when work takes her to the home of late-night talk show host Mi-
ael Williams, his relentless determination melts her cool.

IDDEN AGENDA, by Rochelle Alers (0-7860-0384-7, $4.99/$6.50)
o regain her son from a vengeful father, Eve Blackwell places her trust in
angerous and irresistible Matt Sterling to rescue her abducted son. He accepts
is last job before he turns a new leaf and becomes an honest rancher. As
ey journey from Virginia to Mexico they must enter a charade of marriage.
ut temptation is too strong for this to remain a sham.

TIMATE BETRAYAL, by Donna Hill (0-7860-0396-0, $4.99/$6.50)
vestigative reporter, Reese Delaware, and millionaire computer wizard, Max-
ell Knight are both running from their pasts. When Reese is assigned to
rofile Maxwell, they enter a steamy love affair. But when Reese begins to
ece her memory, she stumbles upon secrets that link her and Maxwell, and
reaten to destroy their newfound love.

*vailable wherever paperbacks are sold, or order direct from the
ublisher. Send cover price plus 50¢ per copy for mailing and
andling to Kensington Publishing Corp., Consumer Orders,
r call (toll free) 888-345-BOOK, to place your order using
lastercard or Visa. Residents of New York and Tennessee
ust include sales tax. DO NOT SEND CASH.*

LOOK FOR THESE ARABESQUE ROMANCES

AFTER ALL, by Lynn Emery   (0-7860-0325-1, $4.99/$6.50)
News reporter Michelle Toussaint only focused on her dream of becoming an anchorwoman. Then contractor Anthony Hilliard returned. For five years Michelle had reminisced about the passions they shared. But happiness turned to heartbreak when Anthony's cruel betrayal led to her father's financial ruin. He returned for one reason only: to win Michelle back.

THE ART OF LOVE, by Crystal Wilson-Harris (0-7860-0418-5, $4.99/$6.50)
Dakota Bennington's heritage is apparent from her African clothing to her sculptures. To her, attorney Pierce Ellis is just another uptight professional stuck in the American mainstream. Pierce worked hard and is proud of his success. An art purchase by his firm has made Dakota a major part of his life. And love bridges their different worlds.

CHANGE OF HEART   (0-7860-0103-8, $4.99/$6.50)
by Adrienne Ellis Reeves
Not one to take risks or stray far from her South Carolina hometown, Emily Brooks, a recently widowed mother, felt it was time for a change. On a business venture she meets author David Walker who is conducting research for his new book. But when he finds undying passion, he wants Emily for keeps. Wary of her newfound passion, all Emily has to do is follow her heart.

ECSTACY, by Gwynne Forster   (0-7860-0416-9, $4.99/$6.50)
Schoolteacher Jeannetta Rollins had a tumor that was about to cost her her eyesight. Her persistence led her to follow Mason Fenwick, the only surgeon talented enough to perform the surgery, on a trip around the world. After getting to know her, Mason wants her whole . . . body and soul. Now he must put behind a tragedy in his career and trust himself and his heart.

KEEPING SECRETS, by Carmen Green   (0-7860-0494-0, $4.99/$6.50)
Jade Houston worked alone. But a dear deceased friend left clues to a two-year-old mystery and Jade had to accept working alongside Marine Captain Nick Crawford. As they enter a relationship that runs deeper than business each must learn how to trust each other in all aspects.

MOST OF ALL, by Louré Bussey   (0-7860-0456-8, $4.50)
After another heartbreak, New York secretary Elandra Lloyd is off to the Bahamas to visit her sister. Her sister is nowhere to be found. Instead she runs into Nassau's richest, self-made millionaire Bradley Davenport. She is lucky to have made the acquaintance with this sexy islander as she searches for her sister and her trust in the opposite sex.

Available wherever paperbacks are sold, or order direct from the Publisher. Send cover price plus 50¢ per copy for mailing and handling to Kensington Publishing Corp., Consumer Orders or call (toll free) 888-345-BOOK, to place your order using Mastercard or Visa. Residents of New York and Tennessee must include sales tax. DO NOT SEND CASH.